THE EYE OF THE DRAGON

Suddenly, Robin and Mari saw Sam
Chan's men pushing their way through
the slow-moving Hong Kong traffic.
They began to run and turned up a steep
hill, the road getting narrower, with
stalls crowding in on either side.

But Chan's men knew every inch of
the district. Little by little, the children
were being trapped.

Mari crashed into Robin, now
standing very still and listening.

'There's someone coming,' he
whispered.

The children were well and truly
caught.

This book is based on the BBC Wales TV series *The Eye of the Dragon*, which was also shown on BBC 1. The series was written by Dyfed Glyn Jones, and produced and directed by Allan Cook. The main characters were played as follows: Robin, Daniel Evans; Mari, Mali Tudno; Ianto Rees, Glan Davies; Gwen Richards, Lisabeth Miles; Sam Chan, Huw Thomas; Michael Morgan, Iestyn Garlick.

THE EYE OF THE
DRAGON

DYFED GLYN

BBC/KNIGHT BOOKS

Copyright © Dyfed Glyn 1987

First published 1987 by BBC/Knight Books
Second impression 1987

British Library Cataloguing in Publication Data

Glyn, Dyfed
    The eye of the dragon.
    Rn: Dyfed Glyn Jones   I. Title   III. British
Broadcasting Corporation
823'.914[J]   PZ7

    ISBN 0-340-40914-2
    ISBN 0-563-20568-7 BBC

Printed and bound in Great Britain for BBC Books,
a division of BBC Enterprises Ltd, Woodlands,
80 Wood Lane, London W12 0TT and Hodder and Stoughton
Paperbacks, a division of Hodder and Stoughton Ltd.,
Mill Road, Dunton Green, Sevenoaks, Kent (Editorial
Office: 47 Bedford Square, London WC1B 3DP) by
Richard Clay Ltd., Bungay, Suffolk. Photoset by
Rowland Phototypesetting Ltd., Bury St Edmunds, Suffolk.

To Rebecca, Daniel and Matthew, of course. Also to keep promises to Alice, Siân and Huw, Sara and Stephen.

ONE

It didn't start off as a race.

Robin Richards, a small, wiry twelve-year-old, was riding his Welsh pony Taran on a path that ran alongside the railway when the little engine came puffing past. Left to himself old Ianto Rees, the train driver, would have taken his time. But he had a partner on the footplate – Mari, Robin's younger sister.

'Go faster, Ianto! Let's get to the end of the line before him. Faster!'

Little by little the engine increased its speed, leaving the sure-footed Taran and Robin behind. Red-headed Mari screamed with delight. They would beat her big brother for once!

Mari wasn't allowed to touch the controls, but she made Ianto blow the whistle several times to taunt Robin. The toots echoed back at them off the surrounding hills; the Beacons Mountain Railway ran through some of the best scenery in a beautiful area of Wales. Above them in the distance towered the twin peaks of the Brecon Beacons; closer at hand were the round hills that were home for thousands of sheep and an occasional herd of wild ponies. And everywhere you looked – trees, trees and more trees. The railway line itself followed the side of a high valley, with a clear lake below that emptied into a busy river and soon disappeared beneath the trees. A restful place, a quiet

7

place if its peace weren't disturbed by too much whistle-tooting!

Perhaps Mari had made Ianto toot too soon. As the railway left the lake and began the long climb up to the high viaduct and the tunnel ahead, Ianto's engine slowed down. Robin was catching up.

'Faster, Ianto, faster!'

'Sorry, Mari, this is the speed the old lady goes up the hill.'

As they reached the top and the end of the line Robin almost overtook them. But Ianto, not wanting to take sides in yet another quarrel between his young friends, decided that the race was a dead heat. 'And I don't think your mother would approve of your racing Taran so hard, or of me pushing the old lady like this.'

He looked guiltily across the lake, which was quite a way below by now, at the converted farmhouse where Gwen Richards, Robin's and Mari's widowed mother, lived. It stood an easy distance from the restored old station that served as headquarters for the Beacons Mountain Railway and as offices for Mrs Richards' many other business ventures.

Not that Ianto was *scared* of Gwen Richards. Well, not exactly. But she *was* a strong-willed woman. She had to be, to bring up Robin and Mari after their father, a doctor, had died in a road accident and to continue her career as a successful businesswoman – and to re-open the Mountain Railway and develop it as a tourist attraction.

These narrow-gauge steam railways usually run along tracks first laid in the last century to carry slate, coal or minerals from the hills to the sea. The Beacons Mountain Railway once carried thousands of tonnes of stone. Soon, if Mrs Richards had her way, it would carry thousands of visitors through the green country-side.

8

If Mrs Richards had her way *and* the line was ready in time. The previous summer Robin and Mari had helped the volunteer workers lay the track from the old railway station, along the lake and up the incline to the top of the hill. And what excitement when the old steam engine arrived, all the way from Germany.

It was now the start of the Easter holidays, and Mrs Richards hoped to push the railway on to the most spectacular part of the route, over the viaduct, then through several deep cuttings into the tunnel, and out the other side to the top end of the lake. Mrs Richards hoped the work could be completed before the start of the summer tourist season.

Ianto Rees, the engine driver, would welcome a longer run – he already knew every inch of the track from the station to the hilltop. A gentle bear of a man with sticking-out ears and a happy smile, his name wasn't really Ianto. He was baptised Evan Thomas Rees, as were his father and grandfather before him. But in the same way as Richard becomes Dick and Robert becomes Bob, so an Evan is called Ianto.

Ianto knew that an engine as fine as his deserved a good long run. Built in 1902, the engine was called the Graf, the German name for a Count. Robin had tried to tell him many times that the engine was therefore an old man, but Ianto was having none of that. *Every* engine was a lady. And this particular lady was polished until every lever, pipe, dial, rod, every piece of copper, brass and steel gleamed and sparkled.

That morning Robin and Mari had come with him to the end of the line to help him with an important task. But before they started work, Ianto insisted on having a 'good cup of tea', as he called it. He had an old railway carriage that he used as his cabin, to store his materials and, more importantly, to brew endless cuppas.

As they sipped their tea – too strong and too sweet, as usual – they discussed the latest news. Someone had moved into the Old Manor at last. That was interesting enough in itself – the old draughty, damp and ugly house had stood empty for at least ten years. More than that, the newcomers were monks; even more than that, they were *Oriental* monks.

'They're probably people from the city who shave their heads and wear robes,' said Mari.

'I don't think they are,' said her brother immediately.

Robin was right. Ianto's mother, known as Mrs Ianto, seemed to know everything that went on in the village and in the district, and she had it on the best authority, said Ianto, that the monks were Oriental, part of a sect that had moved to the Beacons for the peace and quiet to meditate.

'But *we*'re not here to meditate,' said Ianto, throwing the dregs of his tea over some weeds. 'We're here to set up a camp.'

Gwen Richards had managed to arrange a gang of student volunteers to work on the railway extension over their Easter holidays. In exchange for meals and a lot of fun, the students, all enthusiasts, were going to repair the track and lay the line. They would be arriving by the weekend, and by then Ianto had to prepare a site by the lake and pitch tents to accommodate them. Robin and Mari spent the day preparing the site, which meant clearing thousands of stones, large and small, from the lakeside.

'Well, it *was* a railway to a stone quarry, after all. They must have spilt a fair amount over the years.'

'And spilt them all down here,' Robin grumbled under his breath.

Mari agreed.

*   *   *

Robin and Mari knew the history of the quarry; it had once belonged to their very rich great-grandfather, Morgan Morgan, who many years ago had made a fortune in Hong Kong and owned all kinds of businesses and properties all over the world, including his native Wales. Their mother, Morgan Morgan's grand-daughter, still had some distant connection with the company, which was now called Morgan Morgan Holdings (Hong Kong). She never talked much about her distinguished ancestor, though. Later that day, over a cup of tea, they decided to ask Ianto about Morgan Morgan, their great-grandfather.

'A great man in his time,' said Ianto. 'I'm surprised that you don't know more about him. He came here, you know. I'm sure he stood right there.'

Ianto told them the story of their great-grandfather's visits to the quarry and the mountain railway. He always arrived in style, in a Rolls-Royce, the only one many people in the village had ever seen. There was always work to be done on the line, and Morgan Morgan, millionaire or not, liked nothing better than to take off his coat and waistcoat, roll up his sleeves and muck in with the other workers.

'What he liked best was to work in the tunnel,' said Ianto, his voice sounding a little bit odd for a moment. 'Once or twice he insisted that he worked in the old tunnel by himself, no one near him – he wanted to feel the atmosphere, he said.'

Robin thought that this would be a good time to bring up another subject. The tunnel. For as long as they'd known it, the tunnel had been totally bricked up, with a small door at the bottom firmly closed with a large padlock and a strong chain. At the end of a long cutting, the bricked-up tunnel seldom saw the sun and remained damp and gloomy. But recently, taking

11

Taran for a run, Robin had noticed that the lock seemed broken.

'Can we go into the tunnel, Ianto?' Robin asked.

'No, you can't. Anyway, the door's locked.' Ianto's reply was unusually sharp.

Robin told him about the broken padlock, and pointed out that they would all be going through the tunnel before long, when the volunteers laid the line.

Ianto still seemed uneasy. 'They'll have hard hats, and lights, and all the equipment.'

'You don't like the tunnel, do you, Ianto?' Mari had noticed his unease.

'To be honest with you –' Ianto looked up from the bright sunshine at the cabin to the dark tunnel mouth, and shuddered '– that tunnel scares me.' The sun went in at that point, and the tunnel mouth seemed darker than ever. 'But it's an old story. My grandfather, called Ianto Rees like myself, was killed there.'

He went over to the engine and polished furiously to hide his embarrassment as he told them the sad story of the roof collapse that happened in 1940, trapping his grandfather and another man.

'Was Morgan Morgan the other man?' asked Mari.

'Oh, no, he was back in Hong Kong by then. No, it was Dai Evans. But your great-grandfather was very generous to the widows and families. Everyone still remembers that.'

In spite of the war in Europe, Morgan Morgan had returned, sealed the tunnel for good, and gone back to Hong Kong. There he, too, had been killed. No one was quite sure how, but by then the war had come to the Far East. Ianto remained quiet for a while, but it was not in his nature to be gloomy for long, especially with so much work to do.

'Yes, a great man, your great-grandfather.'

* * *

12

Mari rode Taran home that evening. She went cross-country back to the farmhouse, but rather than cross the river, low after a spell of dry weather, she let Taran run along the stream – the pony always enjoyed the splashing water and was sure-footed enough to avoid the rocks and soft patches. As she rode, Mari started wondering – if their great-grandfather had been a millionaire, why couldn't they have a pony each? She must ask her mother.

But when she arrived home, ahead of Robin, her mother had not returned from the office.

'Poor mam,' thought Mari. 'She works so hard.'

Gwen Richards was a short, dark-haired bundle of energy. Some of the dark curls were now fringed with grey, and her big blue eyes needed the help of half-specs to read her endless business papers, but she could still get through more work in a day than most people managed in a week.

She seemed in low spirits when she got home, and when Robin joined them for their evening meal around the pine kitchen table Gwen was in no mood to talk. Her mind was elsewhere. But she did her best to answer the children's questions.

'I've told you about Morgan Morgan before,' said Gwen with a sigh.

'But you didn't tell us about the way he worked on the line like everyone else,' said Mari, 'and helped the widows and their families.'

Gwen knew that the children had been questioning Ianto. She also knew that the engine driver thought the world of her grandfather. Robin and Mari had to know the truth.

Morgan Morgan, son of a Welsh Baptist missionary in the Chinese city of Canton, had made his first fortune reclaiming worthless land on the outskirts of Hong Kong.

'There's nothing wrong with that,' said Robin, fascinated by his mother's story.

'Perhaps not,' said Gwen.

But it seemed that her grandfather had become greedy and had moved on from clearing land to buying lightly populated areas, driving the peasant farmers and the small shopkeepers out, and making even greater profits selling this property.

'So they say, anyway,' said Gwen, 'so don't believe everything Ianto tells you. My grandfather was no saint.' She could have told them the awful story of the temple, but that would have to wait until another day, when Morgan Morgan became too much of a hero again. In the meantime they must all go to bed early – Robin and Mari to prepare for another hard day's work at the camp-site, Gwen herself to worry about the letter from Hong Kong that should have arrived a week earlier.

Why couldn't anything be simple? Because of Morgan Morgan's complicated will of half a century ago, Gwen Richards and her Beacons Mountain Railway owned all the track and land right up to the tunnel mouth. But for long-lost reasons, the tunnel and the track beyond, to the end of the lake, was held jointly by Gwen and Morgan Morgan Holdings. Gwen's cousin, Michael Morgan, chairman of the company in Hong Kong, would have to give his permission to continue with the line. Gwen and Michael had always been on friendly terms, and as the line was worthless to anyone but the Railway there should be no difficulty. But to tidy things up legally Gwen required written approval. Work was about to start, and she was still waiting for her cousin's letter.

The next morning a letter *had* arrived from Hong Kong. Gwen tore open the envelope in a hurry. As she skimmed through the letter her expression changed

14

from excitement and relief to bewilderment and then to cold fury. 'We'll see about that!' she snapped.

The letter was a short one:

Dear Mrs Richards,
We regret that at the moment we cannot grant you permission to develop the land held jointly with Morgan Holdings (Hong Kong).

Signed on behalf of Michael Morgan,
Samuel Chan.

Why should her cousin refuse permission? Who was this Samuel Chan signing on his behalf?

One thing was certain – Gwen would have to find out.

TWO

Gwen Richards was still furious as she went to wake the children. Robin, seeing the look on his mother's face, began apologising about the state of his room — he'd tidy it up as soon as he had a chance, but the wiring from his computer had to be like that at the moment, and he was so tired the previous night he'd forgotten to hang his clothes . . . To his surprise his mother just nodded and told him to hurry up, there was work to be done. Mari had come out of her room and had caught the last few words.

'Work, mam?' she said. 'It's not proper work. We'll be moving stones again. And that Ianto bullying us.'

'You don't mean that, Mari. Anyway, I've got a far easier job for you both today. You'll enjoy it.'

Over breakfast Gwen described the problems that had arisen with the tunnel, and told the children of her decision to fly to Hong Kong immediately to sort everything out on the spot. Not just the tunnel, but other things about the running of Morgan Morgan Holdings had been worrying her.

Mari spoke just ahead of her brother. 'Can we come with you?'

She pouted as Gwen explained that it would be only a short, boring business trip. Some other time, perhaps, they could all go there on a proper holiday together. The children were less than convinced as their mother

16

then told them of the job she wanted done that morning.

'You're a good photographer, Robin. And you can help him, Mari. I want you to take a set of pictures beyond the end of the line – to show how it makes sense to extend the present railway, and how the land is worthless to anyone but the Beacons Mountain Railway. I can take them with me to convince cousin Michael.'

Robin brightened at this project. He had some ideas how to make the pictures look *really* miserable – it would have been even better on a wet drizzly day than on this clear morning.

But Gwen would have none of that. 'No, show it honestly, all the way.'

Mari thought about her mother's last statement. If she said 'all the way', did that mean taking pictures in the tunnel? Gwen Richards hadn't really meant that. But as long as they were careful, wore hard hats, and had Ianto to guide them, why not?

Mari wanted to leave immediately, but Robin had to collect his camera and photography equipment. More than that, their mother insisted that they finished their breakfast *and* washed up. Both tasks were completed in record time. Permission to explore the tunnel!

They thought of taking Taran with them, but decided it would be simpler without her. So Robin and Mari ran from the white-painted farmhouse along the gravel path to the railway station. They could see Gwen in her office, at her desk, on the telephone already – the first phone call of very many that day. If luck had been on their side Ianto Rees and the engine would have been at this end of the line, and they could have ridden on the Graf's footplate all the way to the new workings.

Unfortunately, Ianto had gone on with the tents and

materials; he would be back in his own good time, but the tunnel couldn't wait. They both ran along the railway line, timing their strides to land on the wooden sleepers. The countryside looked at its best that morning – the lake below was so still that it acted as a giant mirror, reflecting the trees, the hills and the distant mountains. In spite of his eagerness to get to the tunnel, Robin was a keen photographer and knew a good shot when he saw one. He stopped to line up his camera, and took two or three pictures for his own collection – not for his mother to take to Hong Kong. Both Robin and Mari were grateful for a short rest; the steady slope up to the high viaduct was telling on them just as it did on the train's engine. Mari was just the slightest bit overweight, too – fonder of riding Taran or the Graf than walking and running.

When Robin set off again, jogging along the track up the incline, his sister was determined to keep up with him. Neither bothered to look up the hill in the direction of the Old Manor. If they had, they might have seen a sight to puzzle them – two of the newly arrived monks following all their movements through binoculars, watching, watching . . .

Ianto could hardly believe his sticking-out ears. 'Your mother said you could go into the tunnel?'

'More than that, she *insisted* that we went in. She wants me to use flash, so she can take the photographs of the tunnel with her to Hong Kong,' said Robin, stretching the truth quite a bit.

Muttering to himself, Ianto collected three hard hats and lamps from the cabin and led the children across the viaduct in the direction of the tunnel. The old driver had seemed uneasy when talking about it, but the prospect of actually going into the tunnel was clearly upsetting him. But Robin and Mari were too excited to notice his unhappiness.

None of the three noticed the monks, who had by now moved halfway down the hillside and were still watching through powerful binoculars.

'Are you *sure* you want to go on?' asked Ianto. 'It's not very interesting.'

He was quite right – the tunnel didn't look very interesting. It was approached along an overgrown cutting, tangled with brambles, thorns and weeds. The big blocks bricking up the whole entrance had been slapped up carelessly. It looked dark and damp, as if the sun seldom reached it.

Robin, after taking a few pictures, wanted to photograph Ianto in front of the blocked-up tunnel mouth.

'Come on. It's for a before-and-after picture. I'll take a photo from the same spot when you drive the first train through. Come on, Ianto. A bit to your left. And smile. Smile!'

To the driver, tunnels and trains were a serious matter, and nothing to smile about. But he did his best. If his boss, Mrs Richards, had given her permission . . . He looked down in the direction of the railway station and the farmhouse, almost catching the monks as they crept closer to the tunnel. If their habits had been anything but dark brown, he might have seen them before they ducked behind a tree.

Ianto turned and sighed. 'All right. Into the tunnel, then. All you'll see will be dirty walls and one interesting bit, if I can find it. Then we can get out and start working.'

The lock on the door at the entrance had been broken, as Robin had noticed. Indeed, the whole door was hanging on its hinges. The three pushed their way through the broken door, and in the odd, shadow-making light cast by their lamps they followed the dirty, damp tunnel. Robin stopped and took one photograph with his flash but he knew that it wouldn't show very much. One old tunnel looked like every other tunnel. Scary it was not; boring it soon became. Now and then they heard small animals running away from them.

'They must be rats,' said Mari, her steady echoing voice proving that she wasn't in the least afraid.

'Not necessarily,' said Ianto. 'There are all sorts of little creatures living in and out of these old tunnels.'

Mari still thought they must be rats, and swung her lamp around, hoping to catch one in the light. She didn't realise that Ianto had stopped, so Mari walked straight into his back with a bump.

Ianto was holding his arm up to stop them and pointing. How he could recognise one part of the tunnel from all the rest was hard to tell.

'It's here somewhere. Swing your lamps up here. Higher up, on the left. Higher again. Can you see it now? There it is, the plaque.'

Robin could see something high up on the wall. Mari saw nothing but darkness. Ianto sounded very sad.

'I'll tell you what it says on the plaque – it's for my grandfather and the other chap. "In memory of two brave workers, Evan Thomas (Ianto) Rees and David J. Evans. 12.7.40."'

Robin began looking for something so he could clean the plaque before photographing it. Of course Ianto, like every good engine driver, had a supply of rags in his overall pockets. He set about polishing like an expert. 'Is that better? Can you see it?'

Mari still couldn't see the plaque, she was just too short, and however much her brother assured her that there was very little to see, the more determined she became to see it. In the end Ianto went down the tunnel, shining his lamp from side to side until he found a large stone. Mari could stand on that, see everything there was to be seen, and they could all leave the gloomy tunnel.

The stone he found was perfect – level and even and quite different from the other rough stones that made up the tunnel wall. *Totally* different in fact, as they soon discovered. Ianto set the flat stone on the tunnel floor in line with the plaque.

'Now, Mari, stand on this. Robin, you shine your light so that she doesn't fall off it. Up you go.'

Mari looked at her feet as she stepped up on to the flat stone, then suddenly screeched and jumped off.

'Robin, Ianto! Look at this! Bring your lamps closer!'

In the light of the three lamps they could see writing on the flat stone. Or at least they could *almost* see the writing, and a pattern of sorts. Ianto wanted to take it outside to see it properly in daylight. Robin wasn't so sure.

'Let's hang on to this one and look around. There may be more stones like this, if Ianto can remember how far along from the plaque he found it.'

But Ianto was happy with any excuse to get out of the tunnel. 'Look, Robin, if there are any more stones, they've been there for almost fifty years, like this one. They won't run away in the next quarter of an hour, will they?'

Mari, impatient as ever, wanted a proper look at 'her' stone there and then, so her brother agreed.

'I'll photograph it properly by the tunnel mouth, then we can come back and look for more.'

Off they went, back towards the daylight, hurrying along the tunnel, and pushed their way through the rickety little door at the tunnel mouth. Were they to know it, they came within seconds of surprising the two brown-cloaked monks who'd crept down to the bushes by the cutting. Mari even fancied that she heard a noise, but dismissed it as the sound of the wind in the trees. She'd forgotten how still the lake was that morning; there was no wind.

Anyway, the flat stone was far too interesting.

'It's not a pattern. It looks like Chinese writing,' said Robin.

Mari wanted to know what it meant.

'Well,' said Robin, as he aimed his camera for a good close-up. 'I can *speak* Chinese perfectly, but unfortunately I can't read it!'

'Don't play the fool, Robin,' said Ianto. 'To me it looks more like a symbol than actual Chinese writing. I'm sure we can find someone to translate it.'

Mari had been thinking and had worked out the stone's significance. 'Morgan Morgan must have put it there.'

'What makes you say that?' asked her brother.

'Here's a railway tunnel in the heart of Wales. Ianto told us of a man who used to work all by himself in the tunnel. Our great-grandfather, Morgan Morgan, came from Hong Kong – the stone has Chinese writing on it. That's not a coincidence, is it?'

Ianto agreed with her, but wondered what it meant. Why put such a stone up on the tunnel wall, from where it must have fallen over the years? Robin thought that the stone could be one of many and that they should go back at once to look for more. The tunnel could be full of them – Morgan Morgan might have tiled whole lengths of the tunnel while working there by himself.

Reluctantly, Ianto agreed to return to the spot by the wall-plaque and search for a while. Mari was keen to bring her new-found treasure with her, but was persuaded that it was unnecessary to carry such a heavy lump all that way. They decided to leave it in a safe place by the tunnel mouth, and in they went again

22

to look for more treasures.

The walk as far as the plaque seemed much shorter this time. Starting at the point where Ianto had picked up the original stone, they searched and searched. They found round stones, smooth stones, rough stones and dirty stones. Robin once thought he'd found another flat stone, but that's all it was, a dirty flat stone. Not a sign of another Chinese stone anywhere.

Almost an hour later, with the batteries in their lamps threatening to fade, they decided to give up the search, hoping that the volunteers would find something when they came to clear the tunnel. Just before they left, Robin got his camera out.

'Let me take a last picture. The two of you by the spot where Ianto found the flat stone. And smile, Ianto. You too, Mari. Get yourselves ready for the flash. Five . . . four . . . three . . . two . . . one . . .'

The light was blinding and frightening in the dark tunnel, but a simple flash could never have caused the crashing noise, started rocks rumbling, dirt falling, the tunnel filling with choking dust, blocking out the lights of their lamps.

'The roof's coming down!' screamed Robin.

The children fell to the ground, Ianto doing his best to protect them. Soot filled their eyes and dust clogged their noses, mouths and throats. Ianto felt something fall from the roof, bounce off his broad shoulders and, judging from her cry, strike Mari.

Still the noise rumbled on and on, still the black dust swirled around them, then, in the distance, came a louder banging noise . . .

'Mari, are you all right? Robin?' choked Ianto.

'I can't see, Ianto.'

'Are either of you hurt?'

The children tried all their limbs, found nothing

23

hurting and picked themselves up slowly from the filthy tunnel floor, moving very carefully to avoid any further rock-falls. Ianto wiped the front of his lamp and shone a feeble light through the swirling dust and soot.

'I *knew* this tunnel was dangerous,' he said. 'Let's get out. This way. Follow me, quickly, but don't rush.'

Slowly, Ianto, Robin and Mari moved along the tunnel. When they came to a part that appeared safe they broke into a sprint. By the time they reached the entrance the children were well ahead of Ianto. Robin pushed the door, eager to get out into the fresh air. But the door they'd left open was now firmly shut!

Ianto arrived, puffing and wheezing like one of his own steam engines.

'We can't open the door. Somebody's locked us in!' shouted Robin.

'Don't be silly! Who'd do that? Give it a good push,' said Ianto between sneezes.

Robin pushed, but nothing happened. He stepped back, then charged the door with his shoulder. He stumbled as the door flew open and they were out in the clear fresh air and glorious daylight again! Mari danced around, jumping up and down.

'We're safe, we've escaped!' she cried. 'By the skin of our teeth, we've escaped the tunnel disaster!'

Robin was less excited than his sister; he was more concerned to check that no damage had been done to his camera. 'Don't be so dramatic, Mari. Nothing much really happened, did it, Ianto?'

Ianto took his time replying.

'Well, I don't know. Just for a second I thought the roof was coming down on us, as it did on my poor old grandfather. We all got a scare; I think I was more scared than either of you. But in the end, Robin's right, nothing much came down.'

'Tonnes of soot, anyway,' said Mari.

'Soot and dust – that's right. It could have been this door slamming shut that disturbed it. Funny really, the soot stays on the tunnel roof for years and years, then you get one gust of wind and it all ends up on your faces. Look at you. I don't know how *I* managed to avoid getting covered in the stuff.'

The children laughed, as Ianto had hoped they would. He knew that Robin and Mari had suffered quite a shock in the tunnel, and to pretend that he'd avoided the soot was really quite funny. If anything, he had more on his face than either of them.

'Let's get cleaned up, if we can. Plenty of soap and water back at my cabin.'

On the way to the old railway carriage they discussed what had happened. Ianto wanted to know if they'd heard anything before the soot came down. He said he wasn't sure but that he himself *may* have heard a short, sharp noise. It could have been the door slamming, of course. Robin had heard nothing, but he had been busy counting up to the flash of the camera. Mari said she had heard an explosion like a bomb going off. Perhaps two explosions.

Ianto smiled. 'No, not a bomb. A short, sharp noise, a flash of light even, behind Robin.'

Before they could discuss the mystery further they'd arrived at Ianto's cabin and soap and warm water took priority.

It took a lot of washing and scrubbing and shaking of clothes to convince Ianto that the children were clean enough to return to their mother. He promised he'd take them down on the train when he was satisfied, which he was, eventually. Robin and Mari were in such a hurry, with such an exciting story to tell, that they forgot one important thing. How could they and Ianto have forgotten it? The Chinese stone had gone right out of their minds.

THREE

The children couldn't wait for the engine to stop. As the Graf slowed down at the station, Robin and Mari tumbled off and ran across the yard to their mother's office. Gwen was deep in conversation with old Mrs Ianto, a plump little jolly lady who was as round as she was tall – always cheerful and more often than not singing to herself. Over the years Mrs Ianto had looked after the children while Gwen Richards was away on her many business trips. She adored both of them. The old lady was now reassuring Gwen, who was worried about leaving the children at such short notice.

'You go on with your work in that Hong Kong. Fifteen hours of flying, that's a long way. And then eating your food with those chopping-sticks. I could never manage it. I know I'd starve away to nothing . . .'

Gwen had to smile at the impossible thought of plump Mrs Ianto starving away to nothing.

'Robin and little Mari will be perfectly safe with me. Nothing to worry about.'

At this totally inappropriate moment the children burst in, still covered in a lot of soot, with an exciting, frightening story to tell. Especially the way Mari told it. 'We were in the tunnel . . . the roof came down. We only just escaped in time, with our lives . . .'

Before Robin could offer a more sensible version of their adventure, Ianto arrived. Poor man! Mrs

Richards – always quick tempered – blamed him for leading her children into such terrible danger. He tried to explain, and reminded her that she had given them permission to go into the tunnel, and that nothing much had happened, really. Gwen calmed down eventually, but insisted that the tunnel was to be locked properly while she was away.

Ianto was pleased to hear that. As far as he was concerned the tunnel could be kept locked for ever.

For the rest of the day Robin returned to his task of photographing the railway track, while Mari helped Ianto set up tents for the volunteers. He had chosen a lovely spot, far too pleasant to be included in Robin's collection of miserable photographs. To their left the volunteers, when they arrived the following day, would have the end of the lake emptying into the busy little river. Above them to the right, the railway climbing up the side of the hill and coming to its present terminus. And ahead, the viaduct, towering above. This bridge to take the railway over a side valley was built in an age when the structures were elegant as well as strong. Balanced on tall stone pillars, six graceful arches carried the track high in the air, and the centre pillar was all of fifty metres tall. A tremendous engineering feat, Ianto would say, simply to serve a small branch railway. And he knew that the volunteers, all railway enthusiasts, would appreciate pitching camp below such a viaduct.

When evening came, it was time for Ianto to drive Gwen to the airport. She had Robin's rolls of film with her; they could be developed in one of the ready-in-an-hour shops when she arrived in Hong Kong.

'I don't think I'll *ever* see Hong Kong,' said Robin, helping his mother with her bags. Mari sighed dramatically and agreed with him.

The Volvo Estate left the farmyard with everyone

waving, Mrs Ianto giving two waves to everyone else's one, as usual. Suddenly, Robin remembered. Something had been nagging in his mind . . . they'd overlooked something. Of course! He realised now! The stone! The flat stone with the Chinese symbol. How could they have forgotten it?

'Come on, Mari, the *stone*. Let's go up to the tunnel and collect it. We can get there and back before it's dark.'

Robin had tried to keep his voice down, but Mrs Ianto had heard him. She wouldn't let them go looking for the stone that night. 'That old tunnel's bad enough in daylight. I know things that I dare not tell. You can go there tomorrow morning. Ianto will be back by then. He can take you to look for the stone, whatever that is.'

The journey to the airport and back was a long one, and it was very late when Ianto returned. He certainly had not had a full night's sleep when he was wakened early by the enthusiastic youngsters. 'Ianto! We've got to look for the stone!'

The driver groaned, tried to open his eyes, and failed. He would listen instead. 'Why don't you go and look for yourselves?'

Robin and Mari had an answer for that, unfortunately. 'It's your mother, Ianto. She says we can't go near the tunnel unless you're with us.'

Ianto groaned all the way to the tunnel, then went straight to a pile of rubbish to the left of the bricked-up entrance.

'Here we are. Oh!'

'It's not here, Ianto.'

'I'm sure that's where we left it before we went back into the tunnel. Stones can't walk.'

They spent some time looking around the tunnel

mouth. They searched in the obvious places, the likely places, less likely spots, unlikely spots, and in the end in totally impossible places, but there was no sign of the stone with the symbol. Mari then suggested that they might have left it just *inside* the tunnel, which infuriated Ianto.

'I *know* we didn't. But even if we had, and the stone were made of solid diamond, I wouldn't open the door for you. Your mother said, and she's quite right, that the tunnel stays locked.'

Robin insisted that they kept on looking – he was never one to give up – and it was Robin who found the flat stone, very near the spot that Ianto had indicated in the first place, by a pile of rubbish to the left of the tunnel mouth.

'I could have *sworn* that we looked there,' said Mari. 'How could we have missed it?'

'Very odd,' said Ianto. 'But that's the tunnel for you. Strange things do happen.'

Mari suggested that they kept the Chinese stone with them as they went down to put the finishing touches to the camp. The volunteers were due to arrive during the morning, and if Ianto had his way they would be working on extending the line by afternoon. There was a lot to do in a very short time.

As Robin, Mari and Ianto left the tunnel mouth, two monks crept away in the opposite direction, satisfied that the stone had been returned without arousing suspicion, but still smarting from their telling-off. They had seen the stone when Mari had brought it out of the tunnel the day before, and had recognised the symbol immediately. When Ianto and the children had gone back into the tunnel, it had seemed a good idea, after scaring them with a fire-cracker, to take the stone to the Monastery, as they called the Old Manor. There they could examine it closely, at leisure, and eventually they decided to make an international telephone call to the Master. He was as excited as they were about the symbol, but was furious that the monks had been foolish enough to remove the stone, to draw attention to its importance. Now they had returned it, and were determined to carry out the Master's other instructions – to keep everyone away from the tunnel, by any means.

It was evening in Hong Kong when Samuel Chan heard the news about the symbol on the stone. He was very excited, though little of it showed on his impassive face. He tidied a few papers on his already tidy desk and put on his suit jacket, smiling quietly. His office was on the forty-third floor of a skyscraper on the Hong Kong harbour waterfront – a skyscraper partly owned by Morgan Morgan Holdings. Chan took the fast lift down and examined himself in the lift's mirror. His lightweight suit was immaculate, his tie exactly straight; his fine, strong face was dignified and he looked important. In fact he had not a hair out of place, except that Samuel Chan did not have a hair on his head to be out of place – he was completely bald. This and his smooth skin made it difficult to guess his age; he could have been thirty as easily he could have been sixty. The gold-rimmed spectacles he always wore suggested the latter.

The lift reached the ground floor and Chan strode out of the air-conditioned lobby to the heat, humidity and frenzy of Hong Kong's evening rush-hour. He walked the few hundred metres to the pier where ferry-boats left central Hong Kong for the islands. The colony of Hong Kong consists of Kowloon and the New Territories on the mainland, Hong Kong island itself and other islands, large and small.

Samuel Chan was going to visit one of these islands,

Cheung Chau, an hour's ferry ride away. The boat was packed with many regular travellers reading newspapers, paying no attention to the passing scenery, and tourists dashing about, finding everything exciting. Chan chose to stand at the stern of the boat and to watch the white wake. Someone offered him a seat, but he was so deep in thought he hardly heard, and must have seemed very impolite.

After the endless bustle and day-long traffic jams of Hong Kong, Cheung Chau seemed very peaceful, for the simple reason that no cars, vans or lorries are allowed on this dumb-bell-shaped island. The ferry-boat tied up at the quay of the small town that filled the low-lying centre part of the dumb-bell, and the passengers streamed off. Samuel Chan had pushed his way to the front of the queue; he was obviously in a hurry. Cheung Chau may not have motor vehicles, but it is certainly not empty. The tall Chinese had to weave his way through the crowds of people, the market stalls and the open-air food shops, past the fish drying on lines like rows of washing. All the time he had to dodge the endless hand-carts moving goods from one end of the island to the other – cans of soft drinks, vegetables, gas cylinders, suitcases to the hotels, meats, fruit . . .

Samuel Chan was obviously following a familiar route that took him away from the busy quayside through narrow streets and up endless sets of steps to a mountain path. He was now passing luxury villas behind high stone walls, with bright blazes of colourful flowers everywhere. Near the top of the mountain, with a panoramic view of the town and the bays below, and dozens of other islands, he reached the end of his journey. He had been looking odder and odder as he climbed the mountain, and by the time he reached a large burnt-down bungalow he appeared to be in a trance.

He paused, turned his back on the bungalow and walked down some steps to a small temple. For a long time he knelt silently at an altar set in the wall, then rose slowly and spoke to himself loudly: 'So we've found it, grandfather. In an old railway tunnel in Wales. That's where the devil Morgan Morgan took it. At last! The Eye of the Dragon. I'll bring it back, I swear it. Then your spirit can rest in peace, grandfather . . .'

Little by little Samuel Chan came out of his strange trance. He walked up to the ruined bungalow, sat on a wall and stared out to sea in the direction of Hong Kong and Kowloon. It was there that his grandfather had been chief monk at a temple. Chan had heard the story many times, but he still hated to think of it. He could almost hear the barbarian voice, half a century ago: 'Smash the temple! Smash it down to the ground! All I want to see is a pile of rubble.'

He could imagine the four large Chinese thugs obeying their orders, swinging their sledge-hammers, and the little red-faced man in charge doing his own share of the wrecking.

Chan's grandfather could not resist. His was a sect dedicated to peace and non-violence. They had been safe on this piece of wasteland on the outskirts of Kowloon for years, praying and worshipping and guarding their treasures, guarding them for the Imperial family – jewels, jade, ivory, gold and silver. Most of all, they were the guardians of the Dragon. The ancient porcelain beast was valuable as pottery, but when you looked at its eye, 'valuable' became priceless. Its third green eye, on its head, was one of the biggest emeralds in the world.

Over the years the monks had kept the secret, guarded the treasure. Now the round-eyed vandal with the impossible name of Morgan Morgan was ruining everything. He was making for the Dragon. The chief monk tried to stand in his way.

'I have sworn to guard the Dragon, Mr Morgan.'

'You can swear all you like. You have to move from here. It's my land, bought honestly with honest money, and documentation that will stand up in any court in Hong Kong. I gave you three months to move your hovel of a temple. The three months are now up.'

Samuel Chan's grandfather protested that they had nowhere to go, they couldn't move.

'You'll move!' Morgan Morgan swung his heavy hammer and broke the porcelain dragon in half. A few more swings and the beautiful pottery was like smashed crockery.

Before leaving, the terrible Welshman had collected precious jewellery, including, of course, the Eye.

'This will cover the expenses of evicting you. And don't bother to go to law. No one will take your word against that of Morgan Morgan . . .'

And so it had proved. The temple disappeared beneath yet another of Morgan Morgan's land developments and the Eye of the Dragon was never seen again.

Samuel Chan got up slowly and started the journey back down the hill. He felt refreshed after his pilgrimage and quite pleased with himself. When he'd first come across the trail of the Eye it had seemed a good idea to send two men to Wales to keep an eye on things. And his foresight had paid off. They seemed to be doing their job of keeping people away from the tunnel – the firecrackers that had frightened the engine driver and the two Richards children were necessary, effective and had hurt no one. They'd made a mistake with the stone, though. Yet that symbol in the tunnel proved he was very close to finding the Eye. He was close also to success in the other part of his plan.

Deep in thought, Chan noticed nothing on his walk

down the hill, through the town and on to the quayside. By now it was getting dark and lights were twinkling around Cheung Chau's small harbour. The place was busier than ever as everyone seemed to come out on to the streets to enjoy the cool of the evening. The ferry back to Hong Kong would leave in five minutes and Samuel Chan made his way to the pier. Then he changed his mind, turned around and walked into the heart of Cheung Chau town. Once he turned off the main road into an alley, the street lighting got very dim. But Chan knew exactly where he was going. Half-way along he turned into an even darker, narrower alley and, counting the houses, he stopped at the tenth. He gave a special knock on the door, and it opened a crack. The old lady inside recognised him, for she flung the door open and bowed a welcome.

'Mr Chan. Do come in. The boys are at the back. They'll be glad to see you.'

She led him to a large room at the rear of the house.

The 'boys' were two of the most ugly, villainous-looking types of men. Foo, the taller of the two, had a pock-marked face and large eyes that were continually flickering from side to side. Ling, his brother, was much shorter, but wide and hard. His spiky black hair flopped forward but could not hide a vicious scar across his forehead. Interrupting their game of mah-jong, they greeted Chan. They were both glad to see him, and when he took out his wallet and paid them five hundred Hong Kong dollars, about fifty pounds each, doubly glad. At the moment all Chan wanted was for them to keep themselves available. The time had come for Chan to keep all his contacts on their toes, for he was very close to success with the second part of his plan – after he'd found the Eye of the Dragon he was going to bankrupt Morgan Morgan Holdings and bring the old barbarian's empire crashing down!

FOUR

The temple looked old – six hundred years, perhaps more. It stood high on a headland overlooking a sandy bay. A large building in the traditional Chinese style, its main feature was a long row of wide steps that led from the temple door to the street below. At the moment all was quiet, the only sound that of the waves breaking on the beach far below.

Suddenly two men rushed out of the temple entrance followed by a beautiful, serene young woman. Without warning, one man aimed a vicious kung-fu kick at the other. If it had hit him it could have injured him seriously, but the second man, the younger of the two, swayed back at the last moment, and the kick whistled past. The young man jumped in the air and aimed a blow. Very soon the fight had developed into a full-scale brawl, the two men tumbling down the ancient temple steps. Soon, the older man, who had started the fight, was, little by little, taking a pounding.

At the top of the steps the beautiful woman smiled – she may have been pleased with the outcome of the battle. Step by step the older man was being driven back. He made a final effort to recover his position and failed. After another flurry of blows he collapsed in a heap over a low hand-cart. The young lady laughed heartily as the defeated fighter was wheeled away.

Suddenly a stocky, dark-haired man in a light-coloured suit and wearing dark glasses rushed up to the cart, waving his arms. 'Cut! Cut!' he shouted. 'Cut! Hold everything!'

The ancient temple was in fact part of a film set, and the film director was furious.

'Cut! This is no good. This is meant to be medieval Peking. A *busy* place. But the set looks totally empty. I asked for fifty extras. Does anyone ever listen? Fifty extras, milling about in the background. Where are they?'

One of the fighters explained, reluctantly. 'I'm sorry, Mr Michael – we haven't got the money.'

Michael Morgan almost struck him in rage. He had to admit that money was tight, but had hoped that the Morgan name would allow him some credit. Kung-fu movies were traditionally made on low budgets, but this was ridiculous. Michael calmed down.

'I don't know. Let's shoot the scene from another angle. Perhaps we can make it look less empty that way.'

The actors, who knew far more about film-making than this silly businessman, went back wearily to their positions. But before the cameras started rolling a white Rolls-Royce glided to a stop at the edge of the set.

'Mr Chan's car, Mr Michael.'

Michael Morgan was keen to see the visitor.

'Take ten minutes, everyone. Back on the set in ten minutes.'

Samuel Chan stayed in the car as Michael hurried across to join him. When he spoke his voice was soft, cultured and quiet.

'Well, Michael, how's the filming going?'

'It's going to be a winner, Sam, a real winner. But . . .'

'But . . . let me guess. You're short of money.'

37

'You know how it is. Snags crop up. Temporary snags.'

'All snags are temporary, Michael.'

Michael Morgan didn't notice the sarcasm in Chan's replies. The important thing was to borrow more money, and Sam had never let him down before. Over the years, as Michael had drifted from one unsuccessful venture to another, Chan had encouraged him and helped him out of difficulties by lending more and more money. At a price. As repayment for his loans Chan demanded shares in Morgan Morgan Holdings – mainly for the money but also to gain more control in the company. In fact Michael was quite glad to be rid of the dreary day-to-day business details, to leave them to Chan.

'You see,' Michael continued. 'I feel that I've got it in me to be a successful film director. All I need is a hundred thousand to tide me over. Pounds, that is.'

Sam's eyes widened at the size of the sum but after appearing reluctant for the sake of show he agreed. Michael, after thanking him, said what he usually said on these occasions. 'And you do agree that when this film makes me a fortune you'll allow me to buy the shares back.'

'But of course.'

'It's only temporary . . .'

'Naturally,' said Chan, not believing a word.

Michael was in a hurry to return to the filming, but his colleague had further things to discuss. He had just saved the company a quarter of a million pounds. Michael had been about to give away some land in Wales for nothing. He, Chan, had obtained an offer of £250,000 for it. The anonymous offer had arrived just in time.

'A hobby, that's what the railway is. But as your

38

distinguished grandfather would have said, a quarter of a million will buy a lot of lollipops.'

Michael's protest was a feeble one. 'It's not a hobby, you know. In Wales it's part of the tourist industry. Gwen Richards, my cousin, has worked hard on it. And I *did* promise. She'll be absolutely furious. You've never met her, have you? I don't fancy telling her the news.'

When Chan told him that he'd already sent Gwen a letter and a telex, Michael cheered up. He was more scared of his fiery cousin than concerned about any broken promise.

The bald-headed businessman wished him luck with his filming and swooshed away in his Rolls-Royce. Michael soon became immersed in making an all-action film. Tomorrow, at least, he could fill the set with extras – some on horseback, perhaps. And he would certainly hire some better stuntmen than the present clumsy idiots. After two failures, this *had* to be the film that made his fortune. Thank goodness that his cousin Gwen, still a major shareholder in the company, was safe in Wales, half a world away, and knew nothing of his business disasters.

At that very moment Gwen Richards was just taking off on the long flight to Hong Kong. She had sent her cousin a telex informing him of her arrival time, her hotel and of her intention to sort out the problem with the tunnel, and then to spend some time going through the company's accounts in detail.

Michael did not return to his office that day. When filming finished he went straight to the film cutting room, so it was Samuel Chan who intercepted Gwen's message. The normally cool businessman came close to panic. He had to see Michael, at once.

The film cutting room looked like all other cutting

rooms. Michael was working with Tommy Lin, his editor, who was running the film backwards and forwards at various speeds, then stopping it. Lin would eventually build up what was called a rough-cut of the film. All the while his assistant, Amy, was busy synchronising the sound with the picture and discarding unwanted shots.

'That's not quite right, Tommy,' Michael complained. 'It has to be *perfect*.'

'Then you'll have to shoot it again, Mr Morgan. We can do miracles, Amy and I, but we can't put something in that you haven't filmed yet.'

Michael was furious. But when he saw a white Rolls-Royce arriving at the studios, he changed his tune. 'Spool back, Tommy. Go to the start of the fight sequence we edited yesterday.'

Samuel Chan entered the cutting room just as the big spools of film stopped spinning.

'Just in time, Sam. Have a look at this. Run it, Tommy. Watch the way the hero moves. Sheer poetry. There! Keep an eye on the other one, and now the movement. That burst of violence, the speed . . .'

Chan was unimpressed. 'You may be right,' he said. 'Let's hope that the audience agrees with you.'

He led Michael away from Tommy and showed him the telex. Michael went pale beneath the tan on his weak, handsome face. 'This means . . .'

'Exactly. I don't want your cousin here, meddling and poking her nose into our business. She would never understand. She's let the company go its own way for years. Why should it change? If she knew how much of Morgan Morgan Holdings has gone . . . how shall I put it . . . has wandered away . . .'

Both men agreed that Gwen Richards in Hong Kong, inspecting the company's affairs, was going to cause quite a problem.

Michael blamed Chan. 'It's your fault, Sam. If we'd given her that railway land, or sold it even, she would never have thought of coming here. Why couldn't you let things be? A derelict track, an old tunnel – just because of them you might bring everything down on our heads.'

Samuel Chan did not reply. He could not stop Mrs Gwen Richards from coming to Hong Kong. He would have to stop her some other way. In the meantime Michael would have to be as charming as possible to his troublesome cousin.

Michael Morgan met Gwen at the airport that evening. He took her in a taxi straight to her hotel and resisted all attempts to talk business. 'Let's leave all that for the moment. Book into your room, freshen up and we'll go out for dinner.'

Later, as dusk fell over Hong Kong, they set out in a little boat called a sampan, driven by a tiny old lady in a huge round hat. They glided out into the harbour, with its millions of multi-coloured lights and reflec-tions, and Michael talked and talked of everything but business. 'We'll eat first, enjoy ourselves and then talk business.'

Gwen was surprisingly wide awake after her long flight, and was also hungry and really looking forward to this feast. But where was the food? A small table for two was laid in the centre of the sampan, chop-sticks – as Mrs Ianto had warned her – at the ready. Yet there was no sign of any food on the boat, or any room to store it. What kind of trick was the fool Michael playing?

She soon found the answer as boat after boat drew alongside, offering all sorts of Chinese delights – chicken, beef, vegetables, sea-food, fish, pork, rice, noodles and much, much more. All they had to do was to choose a dish from this boat, a dish from that, to build up a meal to remember. Another boat drew alongside with an enthusiastic jazz band doing its best to entertain the diners.

The cousins talked and talked, remembering happy times together as children on holiday. Michael had planned it that way, but finally the conversation became serious. Gwen didn't pull her punches – Michael had given his word that she could go ahead and extend the line. She had negotiated a council grant, with difficulty; she had arranged the volunteer workers; she had borrowed far too much from the bank on the strength of Michael's word. The railway *had* to be open before the start of the tourist season, and Michael had put a stop to it.

'Is it really you, or is it this Mr Chan who seems to have wormed his way into everything?'

Michael defended his colleague, pointing out that, for example, Sam Chan had negotiated an offer of a quarter of a million pounds for the tunnel – that was why he had to disappoint Gwen. She was certainly impressed, but grew suspicious as soon as her cousin mentioned that the buyer was anonymous and that all the arrangements were in the hands of Sam Chan.

'I think I'd better meet this mysterious Mr Chan. At once. If we went ashore we could meet tonight.'

Michael grew alarmed. 'No, no, don't rush it! I'm sure you'll get on very well once you get to know one another. Arrange to see him tomorrow, when you've got over your jet-lag.'

Gwen agreed, reluctantly.

The next morning, on the film set of the old temple, Michael found it difficult to concentrate on the re-take of the shots in the fight sequence. The actors did their best, but Michael's mind was elsewhere. He was thinking, for example, of Gwen sitting in an office in the Morgan Morgan skyscraper starting to burrow into the company's accounts, as she had every right to. Why couldn't she have stayed in Wales to get on with her railway line? A quarter of a million pounds was peanuts compared with the damage his cousin could cause.

When Chan's Rolls-Royce arrived it seemed a relief rather than an interruption.

'Take ten minutes, everyone,' called Michael.

Samuel Chan wanted to know how the meeting with Gwen had gone. Michael had to admit that it had been unsuccessful, and that his cousin wanted to see Chan. To his surprise Chan said that he was equally keen to see her, after he'd had time to prepare a few things. Then he would make her an offer. Michael didn't understand. Chan explained his plan.

'We'll buy *all* the rights to the railway beyond the point she's reached at the moment. Give her a good sum in addition to the quarter-million we've been offered already. Then she'll go home.'

Michael was not so sure.

'She'll never sell. The railway has been her whole life since her husband died, Chan. She wants to extend, but even if she fails she'll hold on to what she has like a tigress.'

Samuel Chan smiled unpleasantly.

'Never is a long, long time, Mr Michael. You get on with your filming, and leave Mrs Richards the tigress to me.'

He watched the actors fighting for a while, then drove off in the big white car.

As so often in the past, when Chan was looking for a good idea he went to the peace and quiet of the Tiger Balm Gardens. An eccentric millionaire had spent his money laying out these fantastic gardens, with ornate buildings, stairways, trees, fountains and running water everywhere. In bustling Hong Kong many people came there to enjoy the tranquillity. Samuel Chan walked around the familiar paths, one vital question hammering in his head: how to stop that woman? He stared for a long time at the tall fountain in the centre of the courtyard until his concentration was interrupted by a crowd of chattering, excited schoolchildren running up and down the steps. In his day children were more disciplined . . . Chan smiled slowly. Of course! Children. His monks had mentioned two children, a boy and a girl. That was the way to bring pressure on the meddling Mrs Richards. His first idea was to arrange for his men to hold them in Wales, but the monks had no experience of that kind of work. And the children would be on their own territory. No, the answer was to bring them to Hong Kong, *his* territory. Have them near to their mother, yet so far. She would find it impossible to resist that kind of threat. Schemes raced through his mind, practical schemes, and they would all fall into place as soon as the children arrived in Hong Kong. He even remembered their names. Michael had mentioned them more than once – Robin and Mari Richards, great-grandchildren of the arch-fiend, Morgan Morgan. As he left the Tiger Balm Gardens he chuckled to himself. 'Well, Robin and Mari, you're in for a big surprise.'

FIVE

When the exciting news arrived Mari and Robin were helping Ianto put the finishing touches to the camp-site below the viaduct. Or rather they were arguing with him – Mari wanted to sleep with the girl volunteers who would be in the old station building and Robin wanted to stay with the boys in the tents. Ianto would have none of it until their mother returned.

'I'll tell you one thing,' he said, smiling. 'You may not be allowed to camp with the volunteers, but you have my full permission, and your mother's I'm sure . . .'

'Yes, Ianto?' said Robin.

'Full permission to *work* with the volunteers.'

Before the children could stop Ianto from laughing at his own joke, they were interrupted. Mrs Ianto was hurrying along the railway, as fast as her plump little body would carry her.

'Just had a phone call. Let me get my breath back . . . A call, all the way from Hong Kong.'

Robin was immediately anxious about his mother. Mrs Ianto assured him that all was well, but that Gwen would have to stay for several more days. Mari wanted to know how her mother sounded.

'It wasn't her on the phone. Somebody who works for the company, a Mr Samuel Chan. There's a fine name for you. And he sounded such a gentleman. Talk about a clear line, he could have been in the next room

45

– better line than you get when you phone Cardiff or the next village.'

'But what did this Mr Chan have to *say*?' asked Robin, interrupting her.

Very calmly, Mrs Ianto dropped her bombshell. Since their mother was staying on, she'd decided that the children could go over and join her. Ianto would take them to the airport early the following morning, and their tickets would be there waiting for them. At the end of their journey they would be met at Hong Kong airport.

'Isn't that incredible?' said Mrs Ianto with a dramatic sigh. 'Off to the other side of the world . . .'

Needless to say, Robin and Mari were ready to leave hours early. Finally, they were in the car, Ianto at the wheel, with Mrs Ianto waving goodbye.

Mari grew impatient within five minutes. 'We'll be late, Ianto. Can't you go faster?'

'I could, Mari. I could go a lot faster on these narrow mountain roads, with all the bends and the high hedges, and I could run straight into something coming the other way – a car, a milk lorry or a flock of sheep . . . *That* would slow us down. Don't worry, we're in plenty of time.'

But even the gentle Ianto got frustrated when they reached the canal, to be held up by the first boat of the morning . . . But they were at the airport in plenty of time, and all the arrangements with their tickets and passports worked perfectly. The woman at the check-in desk told Ianto that he needn't wait for takeoff. 'We'll take care of them now. It's a fourteen-hour flight, with one stop at Dubai in the Gulf. They'll have plenty to eat and two films to enjoy.'

Robin and Mari were quite used to flying, and the previous year had been to Canada by themselves to

46

stay with friends of their mother's. But Hong Kong was further, and different.

In spite of the meals, and the films, and the choice of music on their seat headphones, the first half of the flight seemed to go on and on. The stop at Dubai to refuel was interesting, especially as it gave them a chance to see many different Arab people in different robes and head-dresses waiting for flights to places with exotic names.

Soon after takeoff on the second part of the flight they both fell asleep, and the next thing they heard was the pilot's voice announcing that they were approaching Hong Kong.

From the window they could see the mighty Pearl river flowing past the city of Canton and then opening out into many mouths as it emptied into the ocean. As the plane descended, Robin spotted Hong Kong island dominated by the Peak mountain. Then came the truly exciting, even terrifying part of the flight. The plane descended lower and lower over the sea and the small islands, then it was over Kowloon, so low that it seemed to be on a level with the skyscrapers; the children felt that they could almost look in through the windows of flats and offices. Robin wondered what the people living in those buildings made of a daily stream of jumbo jets passing their windows and balconies! Then the giant plane banked to the right, and there was the airport ahead of them, the runway a narrow finger of land sticking out into Hong Kong harbour. The plane landed gently and slowed down as it thundered along the runway. All that could be seen from the windows was the sea on both sides. Even though Robin and Mari knew that the plane's wheels were safely on the runway, it was still an odd feeling.

The jumbo finally came to a halt, turned round and taxied towards the terminal building. They were there!

One of the hostesses had already told them what to do.

'Don't you worry, we'll give you an aunty to see you through customs and immigration. An aunty is what we call our ground hostesses who look after children. She'll take care of you until someone picks you up.'

The aunty was called Jane. She took Mari and Robin through immigration control, found their bags on the carousel, and then led them straight through Customs. Soon they were in the arrivals hall.

The children looked around for their mother, or perhaps their Uncle Michael, whom they knew from photographs, but saw no sign of either. Before they could start worrying, Jane was there to help them. 'Look over there.' At the far end of the arrivals hall stood a row of people; each person was holding a placard with a name on it. Most of the names were those of companies, obviously held by chauffeurs sent to collect businessmen. In the middle of this crush of placards there was one small ornate blackboard. Chalked on it were the names Robin and Mari Richards. Jane took them across and introduced them to the large man with the placard.

'Robin Richards, and Mari. They were expecting their mother to meet them.'

The chauffeur smiled and spoke in Chinese.

'He'll take you straight to the hotel, and he's sorry he doesn't speak English,' Jane told them. 'It's been nice having you on the flight – come again soon. Goodbye.'

The large Chinese man put their luggage on a trolley and led Robin and Mari out of the arrivals hall to the parking area. As the children left the air-conditioned airport building for the first time they were over-whelmed by the heat and humidity. Walking to the car was like taking a Turkish bath. But neither complained – they were in Hong Kong at last!

The car didn't disappoint them either – it was a gleaming white Rolls-Royce. Robin couldn't get over the fantastic sights as the big car took them away from the airport and worked its way through the traffic towards the tunnel that would take them under Hong Kong harbour and bring them out on the island.

'Look at that, Mari. And that skyscraper they're building – all the scaffolding right up to the top is bamboo tied together. And look, another plane coming in! Did we come in that low? I don't believe it!'

Mari was strangely quiet. Perhaps she was tired? Robin asked.

'No. I'm worried. Mam should have met us. *Somebody* should have been at the airport,' said Mari.

'Somebody *did* meet us – the chauffeur. He's probably Uncle Michael's driver.'

Mari wanted to know where they were going.

'Well, *he* knows where we're going,' said her brother. 'And he was there at the airport with our names, wasn't he? Why don't you relax and enjoy the views.'

At this point the car came out of the tunnel into the bright light of Hong Kong island. But Mari would not relax. She felt that something, somewhere was wrong. 'Perhaps we're being kidnapped, Robin.'

Robin's laugh was so loud it caused the quiet Chinese chauffeur to turn his head in amazement.

'Mari. Mari. Kidnappings only happen in books. You read too much trash, that's your trouble. We're being taken to our hotel . . .'

The traffic was heavy, so it took another half an hour to reach the hotel. Robin was getting more and more excited, but Mari was still subdued.

'Cheer up, Mari. Mam will be there to meet us at the hotel. Enjoy yourself.'

Finally the white Rolls pulled up outside their hotel, a tall modern building. A splendid fat gentleman in a maroon uniform, wearing a turban and fierce curved moustaches, opened the car door. He snapped his fingers and a young boy, also in uniform, took the bags while Mari and Robin stepped out of the car. For a moment they felt like really important people. As they entered the hotel lobby they looked around for their mother, but were greeted instead by a totally bald man in a very smart suit. He seemed to know who they were.

'Miss Mari, Mr Robin, welcome. A thousand welcomes to Hong Kong. I'm Samuel Chan, your Uncle Michael's partner, and a business associate of your mother's . . .'

Mari shook hands with this charming man, but, stubbornly, she still wanted to know where her mother was. Chan explained that Mrs Richards was very busy inspecting the company's accounts, so she had arranged for the chauffeur to meet them at the airport and had asked Chan himself to settle them in the hotel and entertain them during the day, to show them some of the sights. She would meet them at seven o'clock for dinner.

After unpacking and taking a quick shower, Robin and Mari rejoined Mr Chan in the lobby for a quick trip around Hong Kong. As they climbed in to the back of the Rolls-Royce Robin fitted a fresh film in his camera. He intended taking hundreds of pictures.

Samuel Chan admired his camera. 'The only sad thing is, Robin, that the photographer himself never appears in any of the pictures. You must let me take shots of Mari and yourself, then you'll *really* have something to remember.'

For the next two hours the camera shutter hardly stopped clicking as Mr Chan took the children around the sights. They started with a ferry ride – the ferries go backwards and forwards dozens of times a day between Hong Kong island and Kowloon on the mainland. They don't even bother to turn round; the boats are exactly the same at each end.

Robin and Mari got a perfect view of Hong Kong harbour, with its crowded skyscrapers backed by the Peak mountain, and the different kinds of ships, from junks to luxury ocean liners, from simple sampans to huge container vessels.

When they arrived at the Kowloon Pier they paused to take some photographs of the old railway terminus – it was once possible to book a ticket there and travel all the way across China, Russia and Europe, to end up in Victoria Station, London. Mari, who had cheered up by now, thought that she might have preferred that to flying! They then returned to Hong Kong on another ferry.

At the pier head there, Robin and Mari had a short ride in a rickshaw, pulled by a man, who stood between the long shafts of the carriage. Mari was especially glad that Mr Chan took some photographs of Robin and herself being pulled along.

After Samuel Chan had paid the rickshaw driver they moved on to the foot of the mountain and another of Hong Kong's attractions – the Peak tram. The railway took them at a very steep angle up, up above the skyscrapers, past the lavish houses owned by Hong Kong's wealthy to the top of the Peak, which dominated the central part of the island. They made their way to a platform from where they could see the whole of the busy harbour below.

'Another one for the album, please,' said Mr Chan as he placed the children in a perfect spot where he could see Mari and Robin in the foreground and the harbour in the background. He returned the camera to Robin, and said a very odd thing. 'And now we're going to Aberdeen.'

Robin didn't understand. 'I don't want to go home yet, not even to Scotland.'

Samuel Chan laughed at what was obviously an old joke. 'Aberdeen's a town on the other side of the island – it's a lovely harbour. There are people there whose homes are on the boats – they've been there all their lives. The boats pack alongside one another and people walk across them. It's like a whole town, but on the water. And we keep the company's junk there.'

Now it was Mari's turn to misunderstand. 'Do you have a lot of junk, Mr Chan?'

'It's not that kind of junk. It's the name of a type of boat, specially adapted to sail in these waters. Nowadays a lot of them are motorised, but you must have seen pictures of junks with their spread-out sails. It's almost a symbol of Hong Kong.'

Robin was intrigued.

'And your company owns one?'

Samuel Chan smiled again, but there was something unpleasant behind it.

'*Our* company, Robin. Morgan Morgan Holdings. Michael's and your mother's company. We use the junk to entertain important clients, and so on. You'll love it.'

It suddenly dawned on Mari that they were about to go sailing. What fun! Mr Chan told them that they were going to sail out to one of the two hundred and thirty-six small islands that make up Hong Kong. And to one of the loveliest.

'Cheung Chau. No traffic, no great noise, but I want you to see a temple and a special grave.'

Robin didn't like the sound of that, but as they

stepped aboard the company junk Samuel Chan re-assured him.

'You'll be interested in this – your great-grandfather's grave, Morgan Morgan's, is on Cheung Chau.'

Mari wanted to know how long the voyage would take. Chan wasn't sure. 'It varies with the tides. Lee will be able to tell us.'

A smiling Chinese boy, about Robin's age but slightly taller, had joined them. The bald-headed businessman introduced them.

'This is Lee. His father is the junk's captain, and Lee helps. His family lives on one of the boats in Aberdeen harbour. Lee speaks a fair bit of English, don't you, Lee?'

The Chinese boy shook hands. 'Very good English, Mr Chan. The journey will take approximately one hour. Would Mr Robin and Miss Mari Richards like to fish as we cross?'

Mari was feeling tired and Robin was more interested in taking pictures, so Lee went away to help his father with his tasks.

As he explored the junk, Robin noticed some large cages kept under tarpaulin near the front of the craft. They were a metre and a half long, half a metre in diameter and loosely woven from wood; they were closed at both ends with twine.

Robin called Lee over. 'What do you catch in these?' he asked. 'Fish, shark, giant lobsters?'

The Chinese boy was highly amused. 'No fish at all,' he laughed, 'unless in your country pigs are fish. These are pig baskets. We carry fat pigs to market in them. The pigs can't run around, and they don't get bumped. But I'm afraid that they *do* get eaten!' Lee laughed again. Then his mood changed suddenly.

He took Robin to the side of the boat and spoke

very quietly, glancing from side to side. 'Please. It is dangerous. I must warn you.'

'What, the waters around here, are they dangerous?'

'No, no, Mr Robin. You must be very careful. Bad man. Very bad man. Mr Chan. You must go . . .'

He stopped speaking suddenly as Chan joined them, his bald head gleaming in the sun and a smile fixed on his face.

'You two getting to know one another? Good.'

SIX

Robin and Mari wanted to know more, much much more about Lee's bad man, but for the rest of the voyage Samuel Chan seemed to stay close to them. Far too soon they arrived at Cheung Chau's little harbour, which was full of busy fishing boats. At the last moment the captain's son tried to warn Robin again. 'Please, Mr Robin.'

Chan's shadow fell across them, and he interrupted: 'Come along, now, we can't waste time. We've a long walk ahead of us. Thank you, Lee.'

They left the junk and walked along the quayside. Robin noticed half a dozen pigs, trussed in their baskets exactly as Lee had described them. He wanted to pause to take some photographs, but this time Mr Chan hurried them along. He led them through the town, up the narrow streets and then the steps that led to the burnt-out bungalow and the small temple on the top of the hill. In the heat and the humidity it seemed a very long way, but Samuel Chan kept them moving. They only stopped once, halfway up the hill, to buy some soft drinks.

'For you two particularly this is a very special trip. When you get to the top it'll all seem worth while, I promise you. Look at that, to start with. You should be proud. The inscription on that rock. "In memory of a founder of modern Hong Kong". That's your grandfather, no, great-grandfather, Morgan Morgan.'

Underneath the inscription on a rock the children could see a carved Chinese symbol. 'But that's exactly like the symbol on my stone in the tunnel,' said Mari.

Mr Chan did not seem very impressed. 'What tunnel is that?' he asked. 'Here in Hong Kong?'

The children explained, but Chan pooh-poohed the coincidence. 'The trouble is, if you don't understand our writing the letters – pictograms really – in Chinese *can* look alike.' He doubted whether Morgan Morgan would have a stone saying The Eye of the Dragon put up in a railway tunnel in the heart of Wales. 'That was his nickname, you know. The Eye of the Dragon. Because he had green eyes, perhaps.'

Mari, who also had green eyes, suddenly became secretly proud of her distinguished great-grandfather.

Both the children were convinced that this was the symbol from the tunnel. Mari remembered the squiggly part at the bottom. Robin thought that he could recollect it all. Mr Chan made a suggestion. 'Why don't you photograph it, then compare the memorial with your symbol when you get home?'

The children questioned him further and discovered that the memorial was in fact Morgan Morgan's grave.

Mari then noticed the derelict bungalow.

'What happened to that house? Who owns that?'

'The company owns all this area,' said Chan, 'but we don't repair the bungalow, and no one will buy it either.' He tried to explain the events that were ancient history by now, that Morgan Morgan was killed here, and the bungalow set on fire at the same time.

The children stared at the ruins. Even half a century later the bungalow suddenly became scary. Murder . . . arson . . . an ancestor killed. Mr Chan added to the gloom.

'Many people believe that the place is still unlucky – haunted by evil spirits.'

'There are no such things,' said Robin.

Samuel Chan agreed with him. 'But you know how people are . . . superstitious. And since you don't believe in evil spirits, you won't be scared of the bungalow.'

He thought that the children would be particularly interested in the cellars, which were untouched by the fire. That's where Morgan Morgan used to keep a large stock of fine wines. Evil spirits or not, those had soon disappeared! Chan led Robin and Mari through the ruined bungalow and down some steps.

Strangely enough, the cellar in the derelict bungalow wasn't scary, and it was a relief to get out of the hot sun.

'Do you know,' said Mr Chan. 'Whatever the weather is doing upstairs, the temperature remains the same here. You two have a look around for a while. I have to speak to someone. I'll be straight back.'

There wasn't much to explore in the cellar – some old posters peeling off the walls, rows of wine racks . . . A broken-down old hand-cart stood in one corner, and opposite it was evidence that local people were still using the cellar, superstition or not – a pile of shiny green watermelons, each much larger than a football. The only other thing that Robin and Mari found was a pair of pig baskets exactly like the ones they had seen on the junk and on the quayside.

When Samuel Chan came back down the steps Mari wanted to know about the baskets. 'Did they keep pigs here, Mr Chan?'

'I don't know. Some of the local farmers came here to shelter from the typhoons, perhaps, though most of them are scared of the evil spirits.'

Robin admired the pig baskets and handed his camera to Mr Chan.

'Would you please photograph Mari and me standing by one. We might as well have one more snap as a souvenir of our great-grandfather's cellar.'

The Chinese smiled broadly.

'Better still, what about a joke picture to show your mother? Why don't you get inside a basket with your face peering out of the wickerwork like a little pig on its way to market?'

Robin thought that was an excellent idea – for Mari!

'In you get, Mari. *Oink, oink* . . . plump little pink pig, in you get, there's plenty of room. Just tie the end now. And smile.'

'What you really need,' said Chan, 'is a picture of both of you, side by side. You get into the other basket, Robin.'

Robin wasn't so keen on that, and he wasn't even sure that he would fit, but with a bit of wriggling he was soon trussed up in his basket, side by side with his sister. What a picture this would make!

Samuel Chan adjusted the camera. 'Now try and look piggy. Good. One more, a bit closer this time, just your heads.' He clicked Robin's camera, but nothing happened. 'Oh dear,' said Mr Chan, 'the film's run out. But I know where I can get another one. I'll be back in no time. You stay here.' He chuckled. 'But then you can't go anywhere, can you . . .?'

The fun of being snug inside a pig basket lasted for a while. Robin was the first to get uneasy. 'I'm worried, Mari. Even if he had to go all the way down to the town to get the film, he should be back by now.'

Mari agreed. 'Do you think he's forgotten about us?'

'Worse than that, I'm afraid. I'm beginning to think that he tied us up and left us here *deliberately*. Remember what Lee said about him being a bad man? I wish he could have told us more.' He thought they should wait a while longer, then try to get free.

'Easier said than done, Robin. I can't move.'

'Neither can I. The pigs are trapped in the cage . . .'

Gwen Richards had spent the day in an office high in the Morgan Morgan Holdings building tackling the company's accounts in the company of a powerful desk computer and of Mr Ng, an independent accountant she'd hired to help.

'Let's try the January figures again,' she said in exasperation. The accountant punched a series of buttons and row after row of green figures scrolled up on the VDU.

Gwen sighed. 'January was *meant* to be a good month. But no matter how we look at them, these figures are *not* good, are they, Mr Ng?'

He shook his head sadly. He had suggested to Gwen that she had better look for evidence of fraud rather than bad management. She was reluctant to believe him, but little by little she was coming to the same conclusion.

Some time later the accountant left. Gwen was going to stay late at the office, trying yet again to make sense of the figures. At street level Mr Ng bumped into a totally bald man who was rushing out of a one-hour-developing-service photography shop. The bald man was too interested in studying the new photographs to look where he was going, and didn't bother to apologise.

High above, Gwen Richards looked through some documents in despair. 'Samuel Chan. Chan. Chan, always Mr Chan. If Michael would only give up this film business. The racehorse breeding was bad enough. If he could only see sense . . .'

She heard the door to the outer office open and close quietly. It must be Michael, coming to collect her and to spin some more excuses.

'Michael,' Gwen spoke with her back to him, 'we

must talk seriously before Friday's meeting. And for once you must listen.' She went on to criticise the powerful aftershave lotion he was wearing, stinking the room out. Some fad in the film business, no doubt.

The visitor spoke softly, almost apologetically.

"I'm sorry you don't like my aftershave, Mrs Richards.'

Gwen spun round in her chair to see a bald-headed stranger. Samuel Chan introduced himself. She stared at him for a while, wondering what her first move should be. Gwen decided, as she often did, that the best way to meet a problem was to tackle it head-on. A meeting had been arranged on Friday, but they might as well examine the figures there and then. Chan took the suggestion very coolly.

'You should never have come here to meddle with these accounts. Had you stayed in Wales everything would be so much simpler . . .'

'Simpler for you, Mr Chan.' She accused him of milking the company for years, of robbing Morgan Morgan Holdings.

Chan was totally unmoved. 'Sticks and stones may break my bones, etcetera, Mrs Richards.' He then repeated his offer to buy all the rights to the railway line leading to the tunnel and the tunnel itself, and revealed that he was behind the anonymous bid of a quarter of a million pounds.

'You must be mad, Mr Chan. I'll never sell, certainly not to you.'

Chan assured her that she *would* sell the rights to the railway extension. More than that, she would go home to Wales and forget all about Morgan Morgan Holdings, leaving cousin Michael and himself to worry about it.

Gwen was getting more and more furious.

'Listen to me, Mr Chan. There is nothing in this

world that would make me sell, especially to *you*. Nothing!' The furniture seemed to shake as she shouted the last word.

Samuel Chan put his hand in the inside pocket of his suit and drew out a packet of photos. He passed them to Gwen. 'You mustn't be *too* sure of anything, Mrs Richards. Do you recognise these two little visitors, newly arrived in Hong Kong?''

She couldn't believe her eyes.

'It's . . . it's some kind of trick photography.'

'No trick. Go right through the pictures. You'll see some special ones at the end. Two little pigs, two *happy* little pigs when I left them, trussed up to go to market.'

The two little pigs were certainly not happy by then. They were doing their best to get out of their cages. Mari had rolled over slowly and carefully so that her basket was almost touching Robin's. She tried her best to get her hands to the knots on Robin's cage, but her arms were trapped too close to her side. They were also slightly numb from lack of movement, and this was getting worse by the minute. If one of them didn't get at the knots in the next quarter of an hour or so the task would be impossible. Mari felt like crying at the thought that they would be stuck in the cellar forever, or for as long as the evil Samuel Chan chose to leave them.

Robin cheered her up. 'The only way to do this is to approach it scientifically,' said Robin. 'I need to position the knots on my cage exactly where your fingers are at their strongest. We then have to depend on you, for I can't move my hands at all myself. So you try rolling that way while I wriggle my basket to the left . . .'

'Hurry up, Robin.'

Back in the Morgan Morgan office, Gwen had certainly found her voice.

'You . . . you *monster*. How could you have done such a thing to two innocent children?'

Chan assured her that the children were perfectly safe – for the moment. This was not a good time for Michael to walk cheerfully into the office.

'Michael, do you know anything of this outrage?'

From his baffled replies it was obvious that he was totally ignorant of the kidnapping. And for once he seemed prepared to stand up to his partner. Sam Chan soon shut Michael up by pointing out that this manoeuvre was designed to get Gwen Richards off *both* their backs, that Michael would benefit as much as he did. They discussed the matter openly as if Gwen were not there, and she found it even more difficult to believe that the whole situation was real.

Chan turned to her.

'It comes down to this, dear lady. Sign the railway extension and the tunnel over to me. *Then* the little pigs leave their baskets.'

Her children's safety meant more to Gwen than anything. 'I must know that they're safe, or I'm going to the police. *Now!*'

'No problem, Mrs Richards.' Sam Chan was at his smoothest. 'A single telephone call . . . I've left my chauffeur to keep an eye on things at the . . . at the place where the children are resting. Excuse me.'

He picked up a telephone from the desk, covered the dialling buttons with one hand, and tapped out the numbers with the other.

He ordered his chauffeur to go down to the cellar and to bring the girl to the phone. He could leave her in the basket for the moment and carry her under his arm, she was small enough. Then he was to hold the

62

telephone so that Mari could speak to her mother and reassure her.

If Samuel Chan had phoned his chauffeur five minutes earlier, his plan would have worked. But while Gwen, Michael and Sam were arguing, Robin and Mari were working out their own plan. During the course of his wriggling on the cellar floor, Robin had rolled across a rusty old iron spike, and when he got his basket in the right position Mari found it very useful in loosening Robin's knots. Even so, she had to move very slowly, for the cage was tightly tied and Mari could hardly move her hands. She dropped the spike more than once, finding it again with difficulty, but eventually Robin could feel the top of the basket moving slightly as the knot gave way.

He pulled and pushed and shook and suddenly the basket sprang open. He was free! He crept very stiffly out of his cage. He took so long stretching and rubbing his aching arms and legs that his sister started complaining.

'What about me? Are you going to leave me here?'

Mari, because she was smaller, was far less stiff as she got out of her basket.

Their next move was to get out of the cellar, away from the derelict bungalow, and away from Cheung Chau island if possible.

They didn't get very far – the cellar door was locked from the outside, and the one small window in the corner was far too high. They were free of the pig baskets, but still prisoners. Mari refused to give up. She thought for a while, then told her brother what she had in mind.

'If we put the baskets there in the shadows, when Mr Chan comes back he'll think we rolled over there. He's bound to go over and look. If we hide by the

63

stairs, we can run up and lock the door behind us.'

Robin wasn't very enthusiastic. But it was a plan of sorts, and he couldn't think of a better one.

They moved the pig baskets, and were just putting watermelons where their heads should be when they heard a sound: someone was putting a key in the lock. They were too late! The door opened slowly and the chauffeur walked down the cellar steps. As he came down the last step to the floor, trying to adjust to the darkness, Robin grabbed a watermelon and rolled it towards the man; Mari rolled another. The chauffeur half tripped on the first fruit and staggered around, tripping himself completely on the second and falling painfully. Robin and Mari rushed past him and up the stairs.

Outside they stopped to lock the door. But the chauffeur had the key with him. Mari slammed the door shut, and they raced through the ruins of the bungalow and out of it, searching for the path that would lead them to the safety of the town.

They weren't to know that their mother was at the other end of the telephone, waiting to speak to Mari, to be assured that they were safe.

SEVEN

The chauffeur picked himself up painfully. In falling on the melons he had hurt his left side, his knee and particularly his elbow. He'd also struck his head against the bottom step, and he could feel blood trickling down from his forehead to his eyebrows. His first instincts were to rush out and follow the children, to catch them before they reached the maze of narrow streets in Cheung Chau town. Then he remembered the telephone in the hut by the temple. It would still be off the hook, with his master waiting to hear from him and Mari. The chauffeur had no choice. Reluctantly he limped up the steps, through the bungalow to the phone and confessed that Robin and Mari had escaped.

From the office in Hong Kong Chan spoke rapidly in Cantonese, giving the chauffeur orders to be acted on immediately. Gwen Richards, concerned about her children, demanded to know what was happening. Chan sounded most convincing.

'A slight hold-up, Mrs Richards. There's always trouble with the telephone lines to the out-islands. We'll have both children talking to you within minutes.'

Michael said nothing. He'd understood some of Chan's telephone conversation and knew that the children had escaped. But if there ever had been a time to keep quiet and trust his ingenious partner, this was it.

Robin and Mari ran like the wind down the steep path and steps. They soon got lost in the busy streets of the old town. At one stage they hid in a dark doorway behind a noodle stall to check if anyone were following them. After standing perfectly still for a minute or two all seemed clear – they had shaken off any pursuer. It was a temptation to stay and watch the lady making her noodles. She didn't pause in her work when Robin asked her a question. He wanted to know the way to the quay and the ferry-boats. She smiled and thought of her reply, proud of her command of English. 'Go all down hill.'

Following those instructions, taking the road that led down hill whenever they came to a junction, the children arrived at the harbour.

But two of Chan's men spotted them immediately. At Chan's instructions the chauffeur had phoned to tell them to watch out for the escapees and to prevent them from taking the ferry. The two men were to hold the children until the chauffeur arrived.

Robin and Mari paid no attention to the two tall Chinese men closing in on them. Chan's men were totally confident – Mari's red hair made the children particularly easy to follow as they wandered about the Cheung Chau quay looking for the Hong Kong ferry pier.

Suddenly an arm shot out and dragged Robin behind a pile of fruit boxes, Mari with him. When they got over the fright they saw that it was their friend Lee, the junk captain's son.

'W . . . what on earth . . . what are you doing here, Lee?' asked Robin.

'Get in this heap of boxes! No time to explain. Bad men are after you!'

'I know,' said Mari, as Lee arranged the boxes behind them. 'It's that chauffeur and Mr Chan.'

'No. Bad men are here on the quay. You'll be safe on the ferry. The one over there. Once the bad men go, you can run to ferry.'

Robin wanted to know if it was the right ferry.

'To Hong Kong. It docks just by your Uncle Michael's office. Please be quiet. The bad men pass now.'

The two pursuers had lost sight of Robin and Mari but had no doubt that they'd soon find the children. As they passed, they stopped and asked Lee a question. The Chinese boy seemed to be leaning nonchalantly on the pile of fruit boxes and gnawing on a sunflower seed. He also managed to cover the slight gap in the children's hiding-place. His answer sent Chan's men hurrying to the far end of the quay.

Lee turned to Robin and Mari. 'Run now to the ferry. It's just leaving. One hour journey to Hong Kong. Good luck.'

'Thanks, Lee,' said Mari. 'I hope that you won't get into any trouble.'

'No time for talk now. Hurry. Just catch the ferry.'

The sailors were about to raise the gangplank when Robin and Mari rushed aboard. The ferry was moving out, dead on time, by the time Chan's two men arrived back at the quayside, shouting for the boat to turn back. Passengers on deck stared at them in amazement. As they put out to sea, Robin felt confident enough to wave at his pursuers, and Mari joined him to wave goodbye to Cheung Chau island. Hong Kong, and their mother, was just an hour away!

In the Morgan Morgan building the tension was getting worse. Gwen, Michael and Sam would look at one another from time to time, then inevitably their gazes would go back to the telephone. Why didn't it ring? It should ring, it *had* to ring. Gwen was about to be very

67

rude to Sam Chan again when the phone went off with a startlingly loud beep-beep-beep. All of them reached for it, but Chan got there first. Michael could barely follow his rapid Cantonese conversation; Gwen understood not a word.

'Where have you been? Don't waste my time. Bring the girl to the phone. What do you mean, you've lost them again?'

Michael and Gwen could hear a tinny little voice explaining. Samuel Chan cut across his chauffeur's excuses. 'You'll be punished for this! But as it happens it could all work out for the best. If they're on the ferry then we know that they're trapped. You bungling fool!'

Turning to Gwen and Michael, Chan explained that there was a slight change of plan. Michael asked his cousin to trust Chan – at which point Gwen lost her temper completely. 'Trust him? Am *I* going mad or is it the world? This man has flown my children halfway around the world . . . He's . . . he's kidnapped them, he's tried to blackmail me, and as for what he's done to the company – yours and mine, Michael . . . And you can stand there and ask me to trust the crook.'

Michael Morgan opened his mouth to speak, but his cousin had by no means finished. She wanted to hear prison doors slamming behind Sam Chan and she was going to ring the police that minute. Chan was totally unruffled. To be called a crook and threatened with prison seemed not to bother him in the least. He put his hand over Gwen's to prevent her from dialling. Calmly he pointed out that if he went to prison so would Michael Morgan, her respectable cousin. More than that, Morgan Morgan Holdings would collapse, including her own substantial share in it.

Michael understood Chan's argument all too clearly. 'Listen, Gwen, *please* listen. Chan has done wrong, agreed. Terrible wrong. But I can assure you that the

68

children are safe. They'll be here with you within the hour. And I have to confess: papers, documents, contracts, agreements . . . I *have* signed them, you know. Please, Gwen. For my sake, for our family's sake. Just an hour.'

Gwen thought for a while. Against all her instincts she had to admit there was some sense in her cousin's plea. Sam Chan took advantage of her hesitation. He promised that Robin and Mari would be delivered to that very room in an hour, brought there in his own Rolls-Royce. He would leave Gwen and Michael to talk. Gwen wasn't happy; she made it very clear to Chan that in one hour and one second she would be phoning the police, Michael's reputation or not.

Robin and Mari quite enjoyed the ferry journey from Cheung Chau island to Hong Kong – they were naturally looking forward to seeing their mother, and this time they could tell her all about their adventure and how brave and clever they both had been. For the moment they could relax. Mari took a special delight in spotting the jumbo jets coming in over the hills behind Kowloon and dropping lower and lower over the city as they approached the airport.

Soon they were within sight of Hong Kong itself with its skyscrapers crowding on top of one another as if they were fighting for space on the waterfront. Behind them the Peak mountain climbed up to the clouds. They'd both been up there, and only a few hours ago!

As they approached the ferry pier they thought they could make out the Morgan Morgan building among the other giants. Their mother would surely be in her office waiting for them.

The crew took no time at all in docking the ferry. Passengers poured off, with Robin and Mari towards the end of the queue. They hurried down the steps to the quay – this would take them to the main street leading to Morgan Morgan's. Mari was looking across to Kowloon when Robin suddenly stopped dead and held her back with his arm. 'Look, Mari. Down there!'

'Oh, no!'

On the corner, at the bottom of the steps, they could see a bald man pretending to read a newspaper – Samuel Chan! He'd seen the children too. He put down the paper and approached. Two men followed him. Chan smiled and spoke kindly.

'Good afternoon again, Miss Mari and Mr Robin. I want you to come with me. I'll take you . . .'

Robin and Mari were going nowhere with this bad man. 'Come on, Mari!' Robin had seen a gap in the heavy traffic on the main road, and they rushed across just as the traffic lights changed and crossing became impossible again.

They could hear Mr Chan's voice above the traffic's roar. 'No! No! You don't understand. Come back!'

Why should they? That was the man who had kidnapped and imprisoned them. What they must do now was to go straight to the Morgan Morgan Holdings building. Mari had worked out the route – a hundred metres up this road, a right-hand turn, cross a street again and they would be there at the front desk.

Then the children saw Chan's men – as villainous as the pair on Cheung Chau quay – pushing their way through the slow-moving traffic, ignoring the cars and hooting lorries, and more than once climbing over car bonnets to get to their side of the road, and in fact ending up ahead of them.

'We can't go straight to the office,' cried Robin. 'Let's go up there. We can lose them and get to Morgan Morgan's building from the back.'

Off they went up a steep hill, so steep that the road

70

soon gave way to steps, and those got steeper and steeper. They also got narrower and narrower, with stalls crowding in on either side. And what a collection of stalls! Food of every kind, household goods, tourist trinkets, clothes, shoes, buttons, locks, bicycle parts, even a hairdresser offering his services, all in the open air on the narrow crowded steps.

It was easier for them to weave their way through the crowds than their big clumsy pursuers, but Chan's men knew the district. Time after time Robin and Mari thought they'd got away only to find a familiar unpleasant face waiting for them at the top of a set of stairs and moving towards them. Every time there was nothing for it but to dive down another alley, up more steps, turn left, turn right. Oh, no! Chan's men again, closer this time. Little by little they were being trapped.

They were finally caught on a set of narrow steps. Looking up, Robin and Mari could see one of Chan's men coming down, scattering people as he walked. At the bottom of the same set of steps, another follower was climbing up. Neither was in a particular hurry, for both men knew that Robin and Mari had no place to turn. At their own pace, Chan's men closed in.

There *was* a small alley leading off the steps, but its entrance was totally blocked by a fruit stall with a huge display of watermelons, apples, oranges and a pyramid of bright pumpkins. Unfortunately, all the produce formed a solid barrier that was far too high to jump. Robin decided to try to smash his way through the pile of watermelons. Mari followed, smiling a sort of apology at the stallholder as the poor man frantically tried to stop all his fruit from bouncing down the steps. She then raced after her brother down the crooked alley, turned a corner and crashed into his back. Robin was standing very still and listening.

'There's someone coming,' he whispered.

Slightly out of breath from running up and down the series of steps was a totally bald man with gold-rimmed glasses – Samuel Chan. And coming up the narrow alley behind them were his two henchmen. The children were well and truly caught.

In the office at the Morgan Morgan Holdings building the clock hand jerked forwards another minute. Gwen pointed at the phone.

'It's been an hour, Michael. So it's the police, isn't it?'

Her cousin pleaded for a slight extension, reminding her of the heavy rush-hour traffic, but Gwen had had enough. She would phone herself. Michael told her that she should ask for Inspector O'Donnell, who owed him a favour or two.

'I want no favours! I want my children back – now!' Gwen snapped. As she gazed out of the skyscraper's window waiting to be put through to the inspector, Gwen Richards saw the reflection of the office door opening behind her, and two little figures hurtling across the room towards her. She put the phone down to hug Mari and Robin, who were jumping up and down with delight at seeing their mother at last and both talking at once: 'Mr Chan met us at the ferry . . .'

'We thought he was going to kidnap us again . . .'

'So we ran away, then he caught us in an alley . . .'

'And he paid the fruit stall man, *and* explained that it was all a mistake . . .'

At that moment their mother was happy simply to have Robin and Mari with her. And she could see that the excited children were also exhausted. 'Look, you can tell me all about it in the morning. Goodness knows when you last slept, so it's straight to the hotel and straight to bed and no arguments.'

For once the children were too tired to argue.

'I'd be happy to take them to the hotel,' said Mr Chan.

Gwen was astounded at his cheek. 'You'll do nothing of the kind. After all you've done. I'll take them. And I'll tell you one thing, Mr Samuel Chan. They're not going out of my sight again.'

Samuel Chan obviously felt back in control again. He smiled. He reminded Gwen that she had promised to sign some papers about the railway in Wales. More than that, she had made a great song and dance about *keeping* promises when she first arrived in Hong Kong. As Gwen hesitated, Chan pressed his case. 'The price is still a quarter of a million, you know.'

Eventually Gwen decided that she had to keep her promise and sign the tunnel away. This would only be a letter of intent because the proper deeds were in Wales.

Chan watched as she signed her copies of the agreement. He would trust Mrs Richards to send the full deeds within a week. Otherwise her esteemed cousin Michael Morgan would start finding himself in trouble, and Morgan Morgan Holdings along with him. Then Chan had the cheek to ask when Robin and Mari were going home, and was there any way in which he could help.

Gwen's look could have killed him. 'Robin and Mari are going home tomorrow,' she said. 'The sooner they're away from here, the better. But, Mr Chan, I think I'll stay on for a while and work with Mr Ng the accountant. Who knows what we'll find?'

The children fell asleep in the taxi to the hotel. Next morning, though, they were both full of beans. Over breakfast they poured out the story of their adventures. Their mother decided it would be better not to make *too* much of the kidnapping, so she agreed with Mr Chan's version of a 'misunderstanding'. She could explain everything when they were all safely home.

Robin and Mari were in no hurry to go back to Wales. And when they heard that Gwen was staying on, their protests grew even louder. But their mother insisted. 'Next time, we'll have a proper holiday, the three of us. This time, please believe me, it's important that you go straight home.'

By mid-morning Robin and Mari were at the airport again. As Gwen waved them goodbye, Robin said: 'You know, mam, I wasn't in the least bit scared of Mr Chan and his gang.'

'You were more scared than I was. Yes, you were,' cried Mari.

Mrs Richards smiled. All was well with her children – they were squabbling again.

EIGHT

Robin and Mari were expected at the farmhouse that evening. Ianto left the volunteers working while he drove to the airport to meet them. As soon as he'd gone, Harri, a happy, plump seventeen-year-old and the chief comedian of the group, stood on a pile of rocks and did a good imitation of Ianto Rees. 'Now you've all done *so* much work today, I'm going to give you a bonus. You'll all have extra. Extra work tomorrow, that is!'

Elin, a tall girl who'd become unofficial leader, tried to push Harri off his perch. 'There's a bit of truth in what that idiot says. We *have* done enough for today. And I suggest an early night for a change.'

Harri had no intention of having an early night. He and two of his friends, Gwyn and Marc, were going exploring. Ianto had told them not to go near the locked tunnel – and that was enough to make them curious and determined to have a look. Gwyn had always fancied himself as a safe-cracker, and with the aid of some bent nails and bits of wire he was ready to have a go at the lock.

As soon as the others had settled down for the night, Harri, Marc and Gwyn crept along the new track, then over the viaduct and into the cutting and finally reached the tunnel mouth. There they came to the first surprise. The entrance *was* padlocked with a stout lock and chain, but for some reason the lock wasn't fastened so Gwyn had no need to try his picking skills. All he had to do was to push the door ajar and wait for Harri, who had the lamp, to lead the way inside.

After they'd walked about fifty metres, very unimpressed with the dark tunnel, Harri put his light out briefly. He heard the other two gasp. Harri chuckled as he switched on the light again. 'Frightened, were you? Afraid of the dark? Or was it ghosts, the spirits of the tunnel, Marc?'

Marc *had* been frightened and was now slightly annoyed. He knew nothing of any ghosts, though.

'Didn't you hear Ianto the other day?' asked Harri. 'When we were in the railway shop? He was telling the girls of some disaster long ago and the ghosts that still haunt this place.'

Marc and Gwyn wouldn't believe him.

'Ask Ianto, then . . .' As Harri said that, he switched the light off again to fool his friends a second time. His voice sounded very echoey in the darkness: '. . . about the gho. . . o. . . st!'

Suddenly the dark tunnel was full of dazzling light as two strong lamps shone straight in their eyes. A voice with a strange accent spoke from behind the light.

'No one allowed in the tunnel.'

Harri stuttered a reply.

'Go now. Don't ever come back,' said the voice. 'Leave the ghosts to sleep.' The strange voice behind the lights followed them as they ran out of the tunnel.

Harri, Marc and Gwyn recovered their courage once they were in the moonlit night. Well before they reached the camp they'd decided that they'd stumbled upon people working in the tunnel who, for reasons of their own, wanted to scare them. After all, there were no such things as ghosts. Perhaps it was worth asking Ianto the story again . . .

A quarter of an hour later the two monks crept out of the tunnel. They checked that the meddling volunteers had really gone. They firmly padlocked the door this time, and they left on a cross-country path to the Old Manor.

At about the same time, Ianto arrived at the farmhouse with two very tired passengers who had still found the energy to talk non-stop all the way from the airport. The next morning he was very impressed by the amount of work completed by the volunteers, but found some of them more interested in talking than in working. Harri took him to one side and steered the conversation to the subject of legends.

'You see, Ianto, last night Gwyn, Marc and myself got talking, and we remembered you telling one of the girls about the tunnel, and spirits and ghosts and so on . .'

Ianto said he knew nothing about it, but Harri pressed him, and after a while Ianto had to admit that there was one old tale, but there was not much to it. Why did the boys want to know? Had they seen a ghost?

'Of course not. Ghosts don't exist.'

'You should forget about all this and get on with your work.'

Harri walked away, looking ever so slightly puzzled.

At the end of another good day's work it turned into such a lovely evening that they decided to hold a barbecue down at the boys' camp-site below the viaduct. Sausages, chops and baked potatoes never tasted better, especially to Robin and Mari who'd been allowed to stay up late by arguing that their bodies and their brains were still working on Hong Kong time. In fact, it was very late when Ianto brought the train along to take the girls to their rooms above the station.

But Ianto was greeted with the inevitable groans and complaints that he'd arrived far too early.

Before he left a voice from the shadow asked about the ghosts again. Ianto was upset.

'Look, sit down, all of you,' he said. 'I'll tell you this story once and for all – that's all it is, a silly story told by silly folk in the village. Everyone around here knows it, so you may as well hear it. Then forget it, for goodness' sake.'

Ianto sat on a box by the dying fire, and the dim red light shining on him made him seem a bit of a ghost himself. Or a devil. The volunteers didn't say a word as he told them of the tragedy in the tunnel that had killed his grandfather and another man.

'. . . and some people say – I don't believe it myself, mind you – some people say that their ghosts are still in the tunnel.'

Harri wanted to know if the ghosts had been seen, but Ianto said that no one had ever seen them. His audience groaned, until he told them what *had* been seen, more than once.

'Right in the middle of the night, when all is quiet and the moon going in and out of the clouds, people say that they've seen their spirits driving a train . . .'

Sensible Elin suggested that people had seen Ianto himself, working late. He probably looked like his grandfather.

Ianto didn't agree, because the locals had always seen the train coming over the viaduct – seen it and heard it. But no train could run where there was no track, and there hadn't been any rails on the viaduct for years. The volunteers didn't *have* to believe the story of the ghostly train, but many people in the village would swear that it was true . . .

* * *

Harri didn't believe a word of Ianto's tale, but in spite of his certainty that there were no such things as ghosts and spirits the three boys who shared a tent did not sleep peacefully that night. About two hours after Ianto had left, Marc started yet another discussion about Ianto's story. Gwyn told him to be quiet and go to sleep. Ianto was pulling their legs, and if he suspected that they even half believed his tale he would come up with an even spookier one.

'Let's *all* go to sleep,' said Harri. 'We agree there's no such thing as a ghost train running over ghostly lines. I'd sooner believe in the Loch Ness monster.'

It was then that he heard the train on the viaduct!

'M ... Marc ... Gwyn. Open the tent flap. Quickly!'

As they opened the zip and looked up to the viaduct, the three friends had the fright of their lives. They could see it perfectly clearly. A train was puffing across the viaduct. They could also hear a slow, steady *puff-puff-puff* and the sound of the wheels clicking along the rails. The cabin glowed red in the reflection of the engine's fire, and an occasional spark flew out from the chimney. *Puff-puff-puff* it went again, steam swirling around. Then it disappeared.

In the dim lights of their torches in the tent, the three looked at one another, trying to make sense of what they had just seen.

Harri spoke first. 'If someone were to ask me I'd have to swear that I've seen a train crossing the viaduct.'

The problem was that the three of them knew that there were no rails on the viaduct, so there could be no train. Gwyn suggested that a particularly large supper combined with Ianto's skills as a storyteller had affected their brains. In the end they agreed to blame Ianto.

As they tried to go to sleep, Marc raised a good

point. 'I'm not sure that I want to face the rest of the gang with our story. They'd only laugh at us. Think what Elin would say . . '

They decided to say nothing and to accept that the barbecue combined with Ianto's storytelling had caused it all. To the sound of a barn-owl and an occasional restless sheep, the three finally fell asleep.

Harri's tent was not the only one that had 'dreamt' of seeing a ghost train. Indeed, the following morning some of the boys decided they'd had enough of working on the railway – nothing to do with the mysterious train, of course . . . No, they couldn't get on with Ianto, so they caught the first bus back to the city.

Ianto had arrived at the site by now, and had been listening for a while, blaming himself for ever mentioning the ghost train and driving the boys away. There would certainly be no more stories!

Up the hill, at the Old Manor, or the Monastery to give it its new name, the monks were busy. A message had arrived warning the monks that an abbot was on his way to join them – a wise man renowned for his deep knowledge of the sect's traditions and customs. What an honour! For the monks it would make a welcome change from their boring task of keeping an eye on the comings and going around the tunnel. Reminded of his work, one of the monks stared in the direction of the old tunnel through his binoculars. He saw no movement, and was pleased. Then he looked at the viaduct, and there he saw Ianto pointing at the track, saying something to the volunteers and then losing his temper as he drove them back to work. This amused the monk.

A little later Robin and Mari took Taran out for her exercise.It was Mari's turn in the saddle, with Robin running along behind. They had decided to go in the

80

direction of the Old Manor. This meant riding up a narrow road with many sharp bends. The journey was usually quite safe, for they could hear any approaching traffic well ahead. But the car that met them that morning must have been travelling at a tremendous pace — it came round a bend like a bolt of lightning. Mari had some difficulty in getting Taran to the side, while the car screeched to a halt.

The driver got out of the car, smiling his apologies. 'I'm terribly sorry. I should know this route better by now.'

The driver was one of the monks, and as he talked the children noticed a very odd passenger in the back seat. Dressed in colourful silky Oriental robes, he stared at Robin and Mari through narrow eyes. The children stared back at his broad, large flat nose and lumpy complexion. The newcomer didn't speak but left the explanations to his driver.

'This is our new abbot, on his very first visit to the Monastery and Wales. You're the children who live in the railway, aren't you?'

The monk asked them about the work, and how the railway extension was going on. Robin replied politely. Before they left, the abbot asked something in his own language. The driver translated.

'The Master asks: does everything in this country, as in ours, depend on the sun and the dawn?'

The children couldn't understand the question.

'Simply,' said the monk, 'what time does your first train run in the morning?'

Mari knew the answer to that. Half-past eight on the dot from the station, nine-fifteen back from the other end. Robin invited them all to come along some time. They waved goodbye to the abbot and his driver and led Taran back down the valley.

Mari made it very clear that she didn't like the

81

newcomers, especially the abbot. 'There's something very peculiar about him.'

Robin didn't like them either, but insisted that they had to be nice to the abbot and his monks – after all, they were neighbours, and they were following their own religion and doing no one any harm. And it was obvious from his robes that the new abbot was an important religious man.

As Robin and Mari walked down the valley, the car completed its short journey to the Monastery. There the new abbot received a warm welcome. The monks took their leader about the building, showing him how the place had been adapted for their worship – a large room arranged as a temple with statues, carvings and burning incense, with smaller rooms as individual cells for meditating and sleep. Then they took the abbot into the garden, proud of the way they had managed to clear away years of neglect and undergrowth to make a tranquil Eastern garden. Above all they had worked on the Old Manor's tower, which had long fallen into disrepair. The monks had replaced the bell and fitted a new rope to ring it. Every hour on the hour the sacred bell rang, its note echoing from the surrounding hills.

'Very good,' said the abbot. 'Very good indeed. A great shame that we shall not be staying here long.'

The monks were too obedient to show any disappointment. They just watched as their Master borrowed the binoculars to stare across the valley. Like the monk earlier, he looked with satisfaction at the tunnel, and then with amusement at the viaduct and the fierce figure of Ianto Rees.

Ianto was leading two of the volunteers, Elin and Harri, towards the end of the viaduct. For the last few metres he led Harri by holding on to the boy's left ear and pulling.

'Right, Mr Harri. You're as responsible as anyone for our losing half our volunteers. So you can answer the question: What can you see?'

Harri, rubbing his painful ear, could see nothing.

'What can't you see, then? Or you, Elin?' The answer Ianto wanted was a railway line. No line, therefore no train. They couldn't afford to lose any more volunteers, which they surely would if the ghost train were seen again.

'I'm going to do you kiddie-winkies a favour,' said Ianto. 'I'll sleep here in the tents tonight. If the ghosties do come, they'll have me to deal with.'

After another hard day's work on the railway, Ianto decided to sleep in his cabin that night – it was near enough to the tents and slightly more comfortable. As usual, he slept very soundly and missed the exciting scene at about one in the morning. But the volunteers saw it – a train puffing its way across the viaduct, and as before the lights, the flickering fire from the engine and sparks from the chimney. And the sounds: the *puff-puff-puff* of the steam engine and the *clickety-clack* of the wheels. Yet the watchers knew that there couldn't be a train on the viaduct!

Harri got out of his tent.

'What are you going to do, Harri?' whispered Marc, more scared than he was prepared to admit. 'You're not going up to the train, are you?'

Harri was going to do no such thing. He would wake up Ianto, so that the driver could see for himself, and pull no more ears in the morning.

He ran to the cabin and hammered on the door. Ianto took his time to wake up and was not in the sweetest mood as he opened the door. 'What on earth do you want at this time of night?'

'Ianto, the train! It's crossing the viaduct again!'

83

'If you're pulling my leg . . .'

'Hurry! Honestly, Ianto!'

But by the time Ianto got down to the camp, the ghost train had gone – no lights, no sounds. Yet looking at the volunteers' faces Ianto *had* to believe that they had seen something. The spirit of his grandfather and his partner?

NINE

Gwen Richards still had problems, mainly now with her cousin Michael. He'd started to see the error of his ways and he wanted to help Gwen in any possible manner. She was getting irritated by the way he wandered about the office, saying loudly: 'I've been a fool, Gwen.'

'Yes, you have. And enjoyed it. What's important now is to rescue what we can of Morgan Morgan Holdings. Otherwise your friend Samuel Chan gets the lot.' Gwen asked him to arrange a meeting with Chan before she left for home, but Michael, as before, was no great help.

'He's not answering the phone. I've left a whole stream of messages. Mind you, this has happened before, many times. Sam has a place on the fringes of Kowloon . . . even the police are reluctant to go there. He could be staying there. He'll turn up soon, though, I'm sure.'

For Gwen, soon would have to be before that night, when she was booked on a flight home. Michael decided to travel with her, to see the property in Wales, and, as he put it yet again, to assist her in any way. His cousin doubted whether he'd be any help, but she was too tired to argue. She asked Michael to phone to let Ianto know they were on their way.

As soon as Ianto received the phone call he went to

the farmhouse, and from the yard called out for Robin and Mari.

'What's the matter?' asked Robin, popping his head out of his bedroom window. 'Have you seen the train in the night again?' The volunteers had given him *all* the details. Ianto groaned; he didn't want to hear about the ghost train. His news was much more interesting – their mother would arrive home very early the following morning, their Uncle Michael with her.

Mari liked the sound of that. She could show Taran to her uncle and get his opinion as a racehorse breeder.

They both wanted to go with Ianto to meet their mother at the airport, but he said no. He would be driving for most of the night to meet the plane.

'I *had* promised to sleep in a tent with the volunteers in case they saw a train on the viaduct tonight,' he said.

Robin looked at him strangely. 'But there *is* no train, is there, Ianto?'

'N . . . no. No, definitely not!'

As Ianto left to get on with the work on the railway, Robin and Mari decided to walk along the viaduct. Today the rails were due to be laid, and they wanted a last look at it as they remembered the track over the years – covered in moss, coarse grass, heather and mountain flowers. Mari found it difficult to believe that anyone could imagine seeing a train when very obviously there were no tracks on which a train could run.

'Ghosts and spirits or not,' said Robin, 'there *will* be a railway line across the viaduct by tomorrow – they're almost there. When they see a proper train going across they'll forget about the other one.'

Mari was only half listening. She had seen something in a clump of weeds.

'What have you found, Mari?'

'Litter. But it's very unusual for climbers to leave it. They're usually most tidy.'

Robin agreed. Climbers had been coming to the viaduct for years, for the fifty-metre drop down the central pillar was a perfect place to practise climbing with ropes. As Mari had said, they were always a most responsible group, not given to dropping litter.

Why, then, should they throw away a plastic cassette case? Careless pop fans, perhaps? Robin inspected the case. This cassette would never get into the Top Ten; the railway shop sold similar ones to steam train enthusiasts. There was always a steady demand for recordings of steam engines, puffing slowly, accelerating or whistling, climbing or going downhill. The true expert could recognise an individual engine from its sounds, so they said. But railway fans were as responsible as climbers; they would not litter the viaduct by throwing cassette cases. So who had thrown this cover?

Throughout the day, working on the line and helping to push it forwards along the viaduct, Robin was deep in thought. The more he heard Harri and the boys chattering about the ghost train, the more certain he became that he knew the secret. But he told no one.

That night, Mrs Ianto wanted the children to go to bed early so that they would be 'bright-eyed and bushy-tailed', as she called it, to meet their mother in the morning. Mari, as ever, was ready to protest, but Robin winked at her. Instead of staying up late to watch television, all three at the farmhouse went to bed – even Mrs Ianto decided on an early night and was in bed soon after nine o'clock.

Within an hour, or a little more, Mari heard a soft knocking on her bedroom door. 'Come on, Mari, get dressed. We're going out,' whispered her brother, entering the bedroom.

'Where to?' asked Mari rather loudly. She had been drifting off to sleep and Robin had startled her.

'Keep quiet or you'll wake Mrs Ianto.'

'Wake Mrs Ianto? Listen to her. She's snoring her head off.' The old lady *was* snoring very loudly, with an occasional squeak like chalk on a blackboard, and bubbling like water running out of a bath. Mrs Ianto was well and truly asleep! As they crept past her room, the sound stopped for a moment, alarming them; then, like a symphony orchestra, the snores returned.

'Where are we going?' asked Mari as they left the house.

'To Taran's stable first, to find a good rope. Then up to the viaduct. I think I know the ghost train's secret.'

Fortunately, Taran made no sound as Robin and Mari borrowed a rope, so the children got away from the farmhouse without in the least disturbing Mrs Ianto. But down in the camp by the viaduct, no one was asleep. Harri and the gang were determined to keep Ianto awake until the train came. Poor old Ianto wanted to catch what sleep he could – he would be leaving in the early hours to collect Gwen and Michael at the airport.

'We *know* the train doesn't exist, anyway. Why wait up for something that's non-existent?' he grumbled.

Harri was right and Ianto was wrong. Within about an hour the volunteers heard the familiar, frightening sound of a steam train puffing in the distance.

'Ianto, can you hear it? You *must* hear it. From the far side of the viaduct – the train!'

Robin and Mari had heard the sound too, and immediately discussed Robin's plan. It involved tying the rope to a tree near their end of the viaduct, laying it at right-angles to the track, and over the wall. The children were by now hiding behind the wall, which

88

at the very start of the viaduct was only about a metre high. Both were holding tightly to the rope. Robin had explained his theory on the way to the viaduct, and Mari had agreed with him, but she still felt somewhat unsure. Her brother was right, he *had* to be; he made more sense than believing in a ghost train. But what if he were wrong . . .?

'Calm down, Mari. The train's coming. Whatever happens, keep your head down.'

The train *was* coming, this time crossing a viaduct with brand-new rails, laid that day. As before, it came in a cloud of steam, lights, reflections from the coal fire and a mighty puffing sound. Down below, Ianto and the volunteers had to believe that something super-natural was happening above their heads, while Robin and Mari, cowering behind the viaduct wall, were equally scared. But Robin and Mari were determined to carry out Robin's scheme.

The lights, the steam, the puffing and fire got closer and closer – more frighteningly by the second. Soon it would be level with the children. It would have been loud enough in broad daylight; in the middle of the night the sound of the steam engine was deafening.

'Now!' shouted Mari, thoroughly scared. 'We've got to!'

'No! Not yet! Hold on! Wait! The rope has to be invisible until the last moment. I'll count. Wait. Five . . . four . . . three . . . two . . . one . . . *Now!*' The children pulled on the rope with all their strength.

Ianto and the volunteers down below had the best view – the ghost train left the viaduct and fell apart. The lights and the red glow scattered in all directions – one lamp was pointing upwards to the trees, another went out while the red light seemed to roll back along the viaduct before coming to a stop, pointing back-wards. All this was accompanied by sounds of things falling and smashing, though the puffing noise didn't stop; it echoed strangely. Some large, complicated structure had fallen to pieces. Before he could run up the steep side of the valley to get to the end of the viaduct, before he could get a better idea of what was going on, Ianto heard someone running to the volunteers' camp, someone shouting at the top of her voice – his mother!

'Ianto, Ianto! The children have disappeared. Their beds are empty. They've been kidnapped, I know it, and I was meant to be taking care of them. What was that crashing noise, Ianto? Oh, the children. Poor Mari. And Robin. They've gone.'

At that moment Robin and Mari were hurrying down the side to the camp, carrying some pieces of equipment. Ianto spotted them in the light of his powerful lamp.

'Robin, Mari. What on earth are you doing there? If you've been playing a trick these nights, then it isn't a funny one. You've lost half the volunteers and slowed the work down. Robin, you wait until I catch you.

By now Mrs Ianto was in tears, relieved more than anything that Mari and her brother were safe and sound. But she knew that she wouldn't be able to protect them from Ianto's fury.

'Hello, everybody,' said Mari as she arrived. 'Did you see what we did, Robin and I? And did you see *them*?'

'See who?' shouted Ianto. 'Don't start playing any more tricks, you little so-and-sos.'

His mother sniffled. 'Language, Ianto. Mind your language in front of the children.'

Ianto tried to explain to Mrs Ianto how much time had been lost because of the 'children's' odd sense of humour. In fact he was astonished that they could be so silly.

He was so cross that it took some time for Robin to get the message through to him that the trick was nothing to do with them. Somebody else, and they had not recognised them in the dark, had pretended to be the ghost train. The children showed them a wooden frame with lights attached, and also a red lamp reflecting off aluminium strips to give the impression of a flickering coal fire. To cap it all, the hoaxers in fleeing had left the stereo playing a tape of steam engine noises.

'*I* found the tape case this morning,' said Mari.

'And then I solved the mystery,' said her brother.

'We tried to trip the ghost train with a rope. If it fell over, then it wasn't a ghost, was it?'

Ianto wanted to know why they hadn't come to him with their plan. The answer was simple. He wouldn't have believed them, would have thought it some further nonsense.

The volunteers congratulated the children – they were relieved that the ghosts and spirits had turned out to be clumsy humans. They all wondered why anyone would want to play such a trick. The best explanation was that the hoaxers were trying to get everyone to stop working on the railway by frightening them away. But why would anyone want to do that?

Ianto tried to calm everyone down.

'There's not much point in my trying to tell you to go straight to sleep, is there? To leave everything until morning? I'll just remind you that I have a long journey ahead of me – to the airport and back here by the crack of dawn. We can talk about it then.'

He reminded them that Mrs Richards, the boss, a fierce woman whom they'd never met, would be with them in the morning, expecting to see a crew of eager and wide-awake workers, not a gang of spookridden zombies with pink little eyes popping out of their heads.

Ianto was still reluctant to praise and thank Robin and Mari for catching the phantom train; he was annoyed that the children had succeeded where he had been fooled. So, rather gruffly, he asked his mother to take them back to the farmhouse and to make sure they slept until the Hong Kong party arrived. In the meantime, he would go to his cabin and soothe himself with a cup of strong tea . . .

At the Monastery the new abbot was absolutely furious with his followers. The fools, the bungling fools. The ghost train was a good way of delaying work on the line, and the monks had prepared the frame, the lights and the sound-system well. And then, somehow, they had tripped and bungled it on the last, vital night. How could they have tripped over a tree root, stone, clump of moss or whatever it was? Were they sure they had not been recognised? His followers were obviously shaken, physically and mentally, but the abbot would not allow them to rest. They all had to go out into the night once again and go into the tunnel, to a special spot in the tunnel. This time things had better be right. And before morning the Master had more work for them. More than that, because of their inefficiency, the abbot, newly arrived, would have to arrange for them to disappear from the Beacons, just in case the children had recognised them on the viaduct.

Time was getting short, too short by far . . .

Under a bright, clear moon the abbot returned to the Old Manor, a box under his arm. The monks were still feeling the weight of his anger, but they thought they could see a contented smile on his large, flat face. Yet when he ordered them to set up the next task they knew that it was not the wish of a contented man. No, here was someone who was determined to gain revenge, to punish his enemies. The monks looked at one another, and each remembered his vows. The abbot must be obeyed.

Soon afterwards the monks bade farewell to their leader and left the Monastery for the last time. The next half an hour was going to be extremely difficult. They had to get to the bottom of the tall central pillar of the high viaduct, and get there in total secrecy. Unfortunately, the volunteers in their camp were still half awake: following the excitement of the collapse of the ghost train, they were discussing the mysterious events. The only obvious path to the base of the pillar passed right by the camp, so that route was impossible. The monks stood by the side of the valley for a while, and came to a decision.

There was only one way to get to their target, and that was straight down. Again the monks walked along the viaduct, this time without their elaborate ghost train apparatus. Halfway across there should be ropes dangling over the edge, dropping down to the bottom, left by the people who came to practise climbing. The monks' worry was that the arrival of the railway line that day might have persuaded the climbers to take the ropes away. It would have been helpful to shine a light, but the monks didn't dare because of the camp below. But the dangling ropes were clear enough in the moonlight as they fell straight down the side. Neither of the two monks had tried dropping down a rope, hand over hand, before, and knew nothing of the technique, though they had watched people do it through their binoculars. Experts would be reluctant to bounce down an unknown face, at night, especially when dressed in clumsy thick robes. But the monks didn't hesitate.

Over the side they went, their hands slipping along their ropes, their feet bouncing off the central tall

93

pillar. They reached the bottom safely and surprisingly quickly – more than that, without disturbing the volunteers' camp in the least. The great worry was the important package strapped on the back of one of the monks. Was it unharmed?

It seemed intact, though the monk had bumped it slightly during his rapid descent. The two men placed it carefully against the central pillar and covered most of it with twigs and ferns. Then one of them looked at his watch, slowly turned a knob on the device, and checked the time that he'd set on the dial. His companion double-checked, and agreed that all was in order. He pressed a red button and the monks left quietly, moving along the river away from the camp. Quietly, too, the package began to tick . . .

TEN

'Here they come!' shouted Robin. He'd seen the Volvo Estate turning down the short road to the farmhouse. 'Mam's arrived! Come on, Mari, come on, Mrs Ianto. Let's meet them in the yard.'

Mrs Ianto thought the children should greet their mother while she put the kettle on to boil.

'I'm *so* glad you're home, mam,' said Robin.

'So am I,' said Mari, and then remembered her manners: 'and it's lovely to see you, too, Uncle Michael.'

Michael got out of the car and told Mrs Ianto that she hadn't changed a bit since the last time he saw her. The old lady was flattered, and led them to the 'little snack' of breakfast she had prepared. The snack was a feast of fresh bread, currant bread, bacon, eggs, sausages, kidneys, fried bread and mushrooms and tea or coffee.

'After breakfast you can all have a sleep. You must be tired. You too, Ianto. Bed for you.'

For once Ianto was willing to agree with his mother's nagging – he had slept very little and driven a long way. But Michael Morgan had other ideas.

'D'you know, Mrs Ianto. We were discussing this very thing with your son in the car. Jet-lag does strange things to your system. Planes fly almost as quickly as the sun around the Earth, and the body's clock takes time to catch up. Gwen and I are wide awake. I'm sure the tiredness will catch up, but at the moment . . .'

Gwen agreed. What she *really* wanted to do, she said, even though it would mean more work for Ianto, was to go for a ride on the train. She had worked hard on behalf of the Mountain Railway in the past week, and was determined to travel on the brand-new stretch of track. 'I know it's early in the morning for you, Ianto, and you must be tired. But just this once, please fire up the engine and take us out.'

Ianto's weariness disappeared immediately. He hurried out to fan the fire that had been smouldering overnight under the Graf's boiler. Ianto was proud to have the chance to take Gwen over the new track, especially since he had been largely responsible for its construction. It was pure pleasure for him to start raising steam in the old engine.

In the kitchen, picking at her breakfast, Gwen was trying to persuade her cousin to come with her on the first journey over the viaduct.

Michael, showing sense for once, realised that this was an important time for Gwen. He would be in the way, he would remind her of the difficulties he'd caused and diminish the occasion somehow. This first journey had to be hers and hers alone. 'Some other time, Gwen. We'll have plenty of opportunity. No, I'd rather go for a walk and a drive. Better still, I could find a spot to photograph the first train to cross the viaduct. Something we can all keep.'

They decided that Gwen, Mari and Ianto would go on the train, and Michael would go in the Volvo to the top of the hill behind the Old Manor. There he would be able to see most of the railway, with an excellent view of the viaduct. Robin would follow him on Taran, taking his own camera. Everyone was satisfied except Mrs Ianto, not because she had to stay in the farmhouse, but because no one had done justice to her excellent breakfast!

All the time, at the base of the central pillar, hidden beneath twigs and bracken, the device ticked away quietly, counting the seconds . . .

It developed into a race between Michael and Robin to see who would reach the hilltop first. The car was obviously faster, but Taran could cut across country and also knew every step of the way. Michael arrived first, and by the time Robin and Taran caught up with him his uncle was staring with interest at the Old Manor down below.

'Someone lives there?' he asked, surprised.

'Taran and I almost beat you,' said Robin. 'Oh, yes. People moved in some time ago. Monks of some kind. From China, so they say.'

That explained the prayer flags that Uncle Michael had seen hanging on a hedge. He wondered what kind of monks they could be. All Robin could say was that there was something odd about them. Michael Morgan was only half listening. He'd seen someone in the Monastery garden and was hurrying down the hill, obviously intending to chat to the monk. Robin ran after his uncle, and arrived just in time to hear the tail end of the conversation.

'. . . and I *am* sorry to have called at this time of day, and disturbed your early morning devotions, Abbot.'

'You were not to know, my friend. Tomorrow you are most welcome to call here, and I will show you our Monastery. Then, there will be all the time in the world.'

The abbot had a very strange voice, sounding as if something was wrong with either his tongue or his teeth. But he bade Michael and Robin goodbye with a warm smile on his large, flat face. Robin and his uncle climbed back up the hill to wait to take their photographs of the train. Michael wanted to know what Robin thought of his new neighbour.

'To tell you the truth, Uncle Michael, he's far more friendly than the other monks who were here before him. When we go round tomorrow, we'll get to know him better. The only thing, I hope he smells nicer by then.'

His uncle looked puzzled. 'I thought I smelled something, but it was probably incense.'

Robin thought differently. 'It smelled more like aftershave to me. A very cheap one, too. When I get old enough to shave, I'll make sure that mine will smell far better than that, even if it costs more . . . Uncle Michael?'

Robin's uncle had turned completely pale and was shaking. Then he stood still, his eyes staring at something far, far away. Michael spoke, each word coming out slowly. 'No . . . no, no. That smell. It isn't. It can't be. It's impossible.' He shook himself and almost shouted. 'You stay here. I must have another word with the abbot. At once!'

Robin reminded him that the train would be there within minutes, but his uncle insisted that he had to go back down to the Monastery. If the train came, Robin was to take the photographs.

Off Michael Morgan went, down the hill once again, walking quicker and quicker, and by the end running as fast as his legs could carry him.

Robin was greatly tempted to follow his uncle to try to understand what was going on. Then he heard a sound that drove monks, smells and everything else out of his mind – from the other side of the valley he heard the sound of the Graf's whistle. The noise echoed from hill to hill. Obviously Ianto had got the engine to full steam, and was now telling the world that the Beacons Railway was ready to start on its first journey over the new track. On board for the first trip would be Mrs Richards, proprietor, Miss Mari Richards, daughter of same, not forgetting Mr Ianto Rees, railway engineer and driver.

Robin *had* to stay on the hilltop, ready to take the once-in-a-lifetime photographs. He knew that there was quite enough time for him to run down to the Old Manor and back before the train got anywhere near, but it was better to be sure and stay there with his cameras. But why on earth would Uncle Michael want to see the abbot again, and in such a hurry?

Michael Morgan had to bang the heavy iron knocker for a long time before the abbot came to open the Monastery door.

'Oh! It's you again. Did you leave something behind? I'm sure it could have waited until our meeting tomorrow.'

Michael didn't reply. He stared at the abbot's face, trying to look into his eyes. Then he moved very close to the Monastery's new leader, bent his head down and sniffed. At that point Michael knew that his nephew was right – the abbot *did* smell strongly of aftershave, which leapt out at him in the clean air of the mountains.

Michael Morgan stepped back, sniffed again, and spoke: 'I have never seen you before. I don't know your face. But I know that only one man wears that particular perfume, a fool who has it made exclusively, and yet ends up smelling like a man splashed with the cheapest perfume. I should know it. I've smelled it for long enough. And it's no wonder it stinks, when the man wearing it stinks too. You do, don't you, Sam?'

Before his eyes, Michael had to witness a horrendous scene. The 'abbot' put his fingers to the skin by his

99

right ear and started tugging slowly. Like a rotten orange, bit by bit, the skin on the holy man's face peeled off! With an unpleasant sucking sound, a plastic mask came away, streams of compound still sticking to his face or pulling away with the mask. There, facing Michael, was his old friend from Hong Kong, now his worst enemy – Samuel Chan!

The Chinese man cleared a few strips of plastic from his face and seemed very amused by Michael's panic. 'No, Michael, you're not dreaming. It *is* Chan. A great shame I have to shave twice a day to keep the mask comfortable. And an even greater shame that you had to come to Wales to interfere. I was certain that the mask would be enough to fool Gwen and her children if I happened to meet them, or anyone else for that matter. So why did it have to be *you*?'

Chan, dressed in the abbot's robes, was quite menacing, but Michael by now was determined to resist him. 'What are you doing in Wales, Chan?'

'What I'm doing is bringing to its conclusion a burden placed upon me by my grandfather. Keeping faith with an oath made half a century ago. Your devil of a grandfather, Morgan Morgan, plundered a temple on the outskirts of Hong Kong and thought nothing of it. He was cruel and callous to a peaceful sect of monks, especially so with *my* grandfather, the chief monk. When Morgan Morgan stole the holy treasure, the Eye of the Dragon, it broke my grandfather's heart. The poor man searched for the Eye for the rest of his life, as did my father after him, pretending to be a faithful servant of Morgan Morgan Holdings to keep close to the enemy. My father had also vowed to get the emerald back.'

Michael Morgan sat down. The strength of feeling from this Sam Chan he'd never known before was over-powering.

Chan sat down opposite him, and spoke very quietly. 'When I was quite young, I was taken by my father to a temple in Hong Kong and had to swear an oath that I, too, would dedicate my life to finding the Eye of the Dragon. And believe me, Michael, that is what I have been doing over the years.'

Samuel Chan got up and moved into the Manor. Michael was impressed by the story, and yet did not feel guilty on behalf of his family, for a wrong committed fifty years ago.

'Why didn't you ask me, Chan? I could have helped.'

'Oh no, Michael. Finding the Eye was only the first part of my vow. The other part was that when I grew up I would use all my skills and talents to ruin Morgan Morgan Holdings once and for all. As you know, I've got very close to doing so.'

Michael ignored that and went back to the subject of the holy emerald. 'And what has happened to the Eye now?'

'Come with me, Mr Michael Morgan, you important man in Hong Kong and Wales. I have something to show you. It's strange how all things come together, end up in the same place, at the same time . . .'

As the former partners walked through the corridors of the old mansion, neither heard a double whistle from the train . . .

Samuel Chan opened the square reinforced steel box slowly. Michael was not allowed to touch, only to look and to admire. He saw dozens and dozens of valuable gems. They shimmered and sparkled even in the dim light of the storehouse in the Monastery's basement. Chan ran his fingers through the treasure, held a handful of gemstones up to his face, and started talking, talking, as if he couldn't stop.

'You of all people should know the story, Michael. I found the first clue to the secret in some papers that

101

came from you — I think it was in exchange for the yacht-building business.'

Michael didn't understand.

'Along with the shares and the rights, there were references to some tunnel in Wales. And they mentioned the Eye.'

Chan dug into the steel box, and shaking lesser treasures aside brought out the giant emerald. It was bigger than an egg and burnt with a green fire deep inside it.

'The Empress of China owned this once, but revolutionaries were invading her palace. My grandfather rescued the gem just in time and escaped from Peking. We still wait for the Imperial family to come back and claim the Chinese throne. Most people do not believe that they are gods any more, but our sect does. When they regain their rightful place, the Eye of the Dragon will be there waiting for them.'

Sam Chan turned the fabulous emerald over and over in his hands.

'Yes, Michael. Thanks to you and the papers you gave me, I discovered that this sacred Chinese treasure, pillaged by *your* grandfather, could be hidden in a dirty railway tunnel in Wales.'

Michael Morgan felt no guilt at all, but he listened as Sam went on: 'Unfortunately, before I could come here to look for the treasure — the documents were vague as to the exact spot — I heard that another grandchild of the devil Morgan, your cousin Gwen, was going to start work on the tunnel. What if *she* found the treasure? I was too close to success to let that happen. Then her children found the symbol on the stone, pointing the way to the gems. Fortunately, I had already sent men to keep an eye on the tunnel and to keep people away by frightening them in any way they could. By the way, they *are* real monks, and

I am a part-time abbot in the sect – the Sons of the Dragon. But as you must have noticed, I chose the weapons of a businessman to bring you down and to gain ownership of the tunnel.

'Michael, last night the most important night of my whole life, I found the treasure. So, for the record – I'll say it now – your dear cousin, Gwen Richards, can have the tunnel to do what she wants with. She now owns the tunnel, and I own the Eye of the Dragon!'

Samuel Chan snapped the steel box shut, tucked it under his arm and moved towards the door of the small room. 'What I'm going to do is to disappear for a few years. Samuel Chan, Hong Kong businessman, will be seen no more. From time to time one of these smaller gems will come on the market to finance setting up the Dragon's organisation, but no one will notice. Goodbye, Michael Morgan. Once and for all.'

Chan stepped out of the room, pulled the door shut behind him and locked it.

'Chan! What are you doing?' Michael sounded panicky.

'Making sure that you won't follow me in a hurry. This is a very solidly built old house. And the windows are covered with strong iron bars inside as well as out – to keep thieves out, no doubt, but to keep people in, too!'

'Chan, don't be silly!'

'Don't worry. Someone is bound to find you eventually. Robin will probably come to look for you. By then I'll be a long way away – perhaps on my way back to Hong Kong. Who knows? With a new face, a new name and certainly a new aftershave.'

Michael hammered on the door.

'Calm down,' said Chan. 'All it needs is a bit of patience. Remember to tell your cousin Gwen that she can have the whole of the line, won't you? A small detail, though: she and her family have caused me so much trouble . . . difficulties, I felt I had to punish her a little. You see the justice of that, don't you, Michael? Revenge can be a noble, even a sacred thing at times. Debts have to be paid.'

Behind the locked door Michael was getting more and more agitated. 'Sam, what are you going to do to Gwen?'

'I'll do nothing to Gwen. Or Robin or Mari. No one will be harmed. I planned it that way. No, well before the trains start running this morning – at twenty to eight, to be exact, the Beacons Mountain Railway will be damaged for ever. You'd be surprised how little explosive is needed to bring down the viaduct's central pillar, and the viaduct with it.' Chan looked at his watch. 'It's set and counting down. I just wonder what your esteemed cousin will do with her new tunnel when the viaduct is down. Perfect, Michael. No one harmed, but all their dreams ruined. That's what I call revenge.'

ELEVEN

'Chan! Chan!' Michael screamed. But Chan had left before his former partner could warn him that a train *would* be on the viaduct. Michael pounded on the stout old door in vain. He tried charging it with his shoulder over and over again, but all he did was to hurt himself. He then tried the bars on the windows, equally unsuccessfully. What could he do? He could imagine the train with Gwen, Mari and Ianto crossing the viaduct, the bomb exploding . . . He knew that Chan, for all his villainy, didn't want that. The train had to be stopped. But how?

On top of the hill Robin was getting more and more uneasy. His uncle should be back by now, however interesting his conversation with the monks. Then Robin saw someone coming out of the Monastery. At last! No. It wasn't Uncle Michael, but the abbot, who went straight to his car and drove away at great speed, his screeching tyres throwing up loose chippings as he left. Something was wrong. If he missed taking any photographs of the train, so be it. Robin had to go down to the Old Manor to see what had happened. Riding Taran, it took only a few seconds to reach the open front door.

The first thing he saw as he walked in, rather nervously, were telephone wires torn from the wall. All was quiet, and there was a strange, dead feeling. Robin wandered from room to room in the large old house and finally heard a distant noise, a hammering sound.

In no time at all he was by the door, but could do nothing to help his uncle.

'The door's locked, Uncle Michael.'

'Try the window, then, Robin. It's urgent. I can't get at the bars from here. Hurry!'

Robin ran out of the Old Manor and round to the back, looking for the window from the outside. Michael kept calling, and that helped. Finally Robin decided that a low, dark window at ground level, half hidden behind a central-heating oil tank, was the vital one. He got hold of the bars and pulled and pulled harder than he'd ever done in his life. It proved surprisingly easy. The bars may have looked solid, but the iron had rusted. In no time the outside bars were bent back. Next, Robin had to open the window. This was not so easy – it hadn't been open for years; it had simply been painted over and over.

Calling on his uncle to stand back, Robin put his foot through the glass, kicking and kicking until a clean hole was left. Now only the inside bars remained.

'Hurry, Robin, please hurry,' said Michael. 'I'll push, you pull. I must get out.'

But the inside bars had not been rotted by the wind and the rain and the mountain weather. In spite of all their efforts, nothing moved. Robin ran back into the Manor, remembering the rope that the monks had tied to the bell in the tower. He cut off a long piece and rushed to the window, where Michael was getting more and more desperate. Robin called Taran over, tied one end of the rope to one of the bars, the other to the saddle. Between his own strength and that of the pony the bar popped out! After that it was no trouble to pull out another and make enough room for his uncle to climb out. He couldn't understand Michael's first question: 'The train, Robin! Has it left yet?'

'Just started, Uncle Michael.'

'It has to be stopped before it reaches the viaduct. Let's go in the car. There's no time to explain.' He looked at his watch. 'We've got to stop that train before seven-forty.'

If Michael had been thinking normally, he would have saved time by calling Robin through the window and sending *him* to stop the train. But all he could think of was driving down to stop the train somehow.

Robin wouldn't go in the car with him. 'You'll never get down there in time, Uncle. Surely you remember the winding road. There's only one way of stopping the train, and it will be very much touch and go. Taran and I will go cross-country. With luck . . .'

'You'll get there. Go at once. Stop the train before it reaches the viaduct. I'm going after Sam Chan.'

Robin was totally confused. Sam Chan, the kidnapper, the pig basket man, here in Wales? Michael had no time to explain.

'Later, Robin. Just stop the train!'

Taran galloped down the hill and across the road, jumping cleanly over a low wall. Then faster, faster down the sloping green meadow that led to a narrow gully with a stream at the bottom. Through the stream, then a struggle up the other side, a long muddy slope. Robin almost fell off as Taran tripped over a tree root, but the pony kept her feet and scrambled to the top. Robin had no need to drive her on; the pony herself seemed to understand the urgency. And the situation *was* urgent. From time to time Robin caught glimpses of the train, or heard its sounds as it came up the long climb to the level part, where it would join the new track to take it over the viaduct.

Bit by bit Robin realised, with a sinking feeling, that

107

he would not arrive in time. In spite of all Taran's efforts the train was going to beat him to the viaduct. At this lowest point the river had cut itself a deep path through high sides. He would have to slow down to take one side carefully, ride Taran through the river for about a hundred metres, and then climb equally carefully up a path on the other side.

Taran knew the answer. Once before, about a fort-night ago, Robin had sensed that the pony wanted to jump across the river, from high bank to high bank, rather than follow the safe path. But the jump was far too dangerous, and Robin had refused to allow such a move. Yet, if they *did* jump the chasm they could save invaluable minutes . . .

Taran galloped faster and faster towards the edge, held herself back until the last possible second, then jumped. They landed on the far side with a metre and more in hand!

There was still a way to go, and they only just caught the train. Ianto, driving, couldn't understand why Robin was rushing past, waving his arms like a fool, and driving Taran harder than he should. Gwen and Mari could make no sense of it either. Then Robin started to cross the railway just in front of the engine – backwards and forwards, ever closer. Ianto must have got the message, for he hauled on the big brake, leaving the old engine to blow out steam and skid, squealing along the line with its wheels locked, raising showers of sparks. Eventually it stopped, about a quar-ter of the way along the viaduct.

Robin's mother wasn't pleased. 'What on earth are you doing, spoiling our first journey?'

He had no real explanation.

'I don't know. Uncle Michael insisted that I stopped the train, after he saw Mr Chan . . .'

Before anyone could ask a question, below them

came a flash of fire and a loud explosion, throwing clouds of smoke and shaking everything.

Above the sound of the car engine, Michael heard the explosion in the distance. He was driving Gwen's car as hard as he could, travelling far too quickly on narrow mountain roads and hoping that a milk lorry or a tractor would not be coming in the opposite direction. He *had* to catch Sam Chan, who was a crook . . . he winced as he heard the explosion . . . and possibly by now a murderer.

Chan heard the explosion too, and smiled. What a painless way of getting revenge on that interfering Mrs Richards. Smashing her dreams without hurting anyone else. And no one could catch him. He would go all the way to London in the car, then fly back to Hong Kong. Then . . . He was hours ahead of any pursuit, which was more than plenty for a Son of the Dragon. He sped round another bend, and had to stamp down hard on the brake. What on earth was happening? The road in front of him was going straight up in the air. Chan had arrived at the canal in time for the first boat of the morning. The family on board waved happily. Minutes passed. Why couldn't they hurry? Eventually, the bridge went down again. The family all waved at Samuel Chan once more.

He was so furious that he flooded the engine when he tried to restart the car. Chan turned the starter over and over again. It finally fired. But too late.

A Volvo overtook him and turned at right-angles to block his car. Michael Morgan jumped out. Chan got out, too, but before he could say a word Michael had punched him in the face. Chan kicked out, caught his former partner in the knee, and left him staggering on the point of falling into the canal. As Michael fought to regain his balance, Chan, the steel box firmly under his arm, ran along the towpath.

Michael followed, confident that he could catch him. While they stayed on the towpath that was likely, but then Chan left the canal and ran along a muddy path up the hill in the direction of the lake. Michael's breath got shorter and shorter. Chan was well ahead of him at the lake, at the far end of the same lake that ran alongside the railway. Here, waiting for the summer season, floated a row of power boats. Chan looked behind him, saw Michael struggling in the distance and chose a boat. Some would have petrol in their tanks, others not. Chan was lucky. After many hiccups the engine fired, and off he went across the lake.

Michael wasn't so lucky. It took him some time to find a boat that would follow. He set off in pursuit of his former partner, fortunately in a more powerful boat than Chan's. Little by little he caught up, the boats weaving backwards and forwards across this far end of the lake. The sound of the two boats travelling flat out must have been deafening in the quiet countryside, but Michael was determined to catch his man. When it seemed he was close enough to touch Chan his engine coughed, spluttered, and fell silent. He'd run out of petrol!

Chan looked back in triumph, a mocking smile on his face. He stood in his boat and raised the little steel box above his head. 'Farewell for ever, Michael Morgan, you and all the devil's family . . .'

At that very moment *his* boat also ran out of petrol, and it jerked to a stop. The current carried Michael's boat right up against Chan – the Chinese panicked, threw his steel box in the air and as it came down it burst open, spilling its treasure into the depths of the lake. Michael tried to jump across, but Chan dived out into the water and swam strongly to the far shore.

110

Michael knew that he wouldn't be able to catch him, so he sat in his powerless boat and watched Chan reach the lake-side, where he waved mockingly and ran up the hill, looking like a rat in his wet, brown abbot's robes. Paddling very, very slowly Michael finally reached dry land, hours too late to catch Chan.

Later that week, at a party held on the farmhouse lawn, Michael described the incident. By then it all seemed very amusing, especially as everything had worked out almost for the best. Very little damage had been done to the viaduct and its central pillar. The explosion, fire and smoke had looked very dramatic, but the old bridge-builders and stonemasons of a century ago had raised their structures to last.

'And even better, Gwen,' said Michael. 'Chan definitely gave you the whole railway line. I'm a witness to that. There's nothing to prevent us going on now.'

'But where *is* Mr Chan?' asked Mari.

'We'll never see him again,' replied her mother. 'We'll be left in peace to push the railway on through the tunnel.'

'Then down to the lake and onwards,' said Robin.

'Then on, and on and on . . .' Everyone was joining in the fun.

'Down the valley,' said Ianto.

'All the way to the city,' added his mother.

'Then all the way to Hong Kong,' said Gwen, amid much laughter.

Robin was more serious. 'It's a shame about the Eye of the Dragon and the treasure. The skin-divers say that the lake bed makes it unlikely that anyone will find any gems except by accident. The only certain way would be to drain the whole lake, and I doubt if we can do that.'

His mother replied, quietly. 'Do you know, Robin,

I'm not sure that we *want* to recover the treasure.'

Mari didn't understand. 'Why not, mam?'

'The gems seem to have brought nothing but bad luck to everyone over the years. The Empress of China, Samuel Chan's grandfather, Morgan Morgan, my grandfather, and now Samuel Chan himself. No, the bottom of the lake is by far and away the place for the Eye of the Dragon!'